Clouds Go Wild

Edmund Faltermayer

authorHOUSE™

1663 LIBERTY DRIVE, SUITE 200
BLOOMINGTON, INDIANA 47403
(800) 839-8640
WWW.AUTHORHOUSE.COM

First published by AuthorHouse 11/23/04

ISBN: 1-4208-0833-8 (sc)
ISBN: 1-4208-0832-X (dj)

Printed in the United States of America
Bloomington, Indiana

This book is printed on acid-free paper.

Cover illustration by Frances Faltermayer

For Steven

Chapter One

"Not again!" Roderick's father said. "You're going to wear out that phone."

"But Dad!" Roderick said excitedly as he leapt up from dinner for the latest weather report. "We could get eight inches tonight."

Did snow matter a lot to Roderick B. Ringley? That's like asking if honey matters to a bear. When it came to the wondrous white stuff that floats silently down from the sky to transform the world into a winter playland, the kid was obsessed. It led to a series of incredible events that people still talk and argue about years afterward. The arguments last far into the winter evenings, when fires burn low.

On this particular evening in early January, snow was on Roderick's mind more than ever. The winter had been mild so far, with only a disappointing half-inch dusting the day after Christmas. But at last the temperature had dropped and clouds had moved in. Roderick's Snow Watch had gone on maximum alert.

All of which explains why a tall, otherwise normal sixth-grader with blue eyes and curly chestnut hair was now hunched over the kitchen telephone — and driving his family crazy. This was the third straight evening Roderick had jumped up to check the weather.

For the third straight evening his father, who was one of the best-known doctors in town, shook his head. "That boy doesn't know when to stop," Dr. Ringley said.

Once again Roderick's mother noted with a sigh, "He hasn't touched his salad."

Once again his younger sister Cora rolled her eyes and said, "Who cares about the stupid snow anyway?"

Everyone at the table became silent as Roderick waited for the recorded voice on the telephone to get to the part that mattered...

SLAM!!

When Roderick hung up, the whole house seemed to shake. He trudged off and threw himself on a sofa in the den. Dr. Ringley looked at his wife and whispered, "Heavy rain."

Mrs. Ringley followed to the den, almost on tiptoe. As cheerfully as she could, she said, "You'll get your big snow before long, Roderick. I just know it."

"Mom, you don't understand!" Her son seemed on the verge of tears. Far more was at stake, to his way of thinking. Even back then, people were beginning to worry that the world was getting warmer. "The whole climate may be changing," Roderick said gloomily. "Some weather experts say we're entering a new Ice Age. But others are sure the world's temperature is slowly rising. Do you realize what that means?"

Staring at the floor, Roderick answered his own question. "It means that we may never see snow again in our backyard. We may even have" — he shuddered at the thought — "palm trees!"

Most of the time, it was hard to feel gloomy in a place like Lysander, New Jersey, where Roderick lived. New York City was only 45 minutes away by train, and Lysander (population 30,000) was as different from the big city as you could ask for. Big, comfortable old homes, many with wrap-around porches, stood along wide, level streets that were great for bike riding.

But now Roderick could hear the rain beginning. Tomorrow the town would be damp and gray and dead. Talk about frustration! Roderick wondered if he would go out of his mind.

Before anything like that could happen the front doorbell rang, not once but twice.

The rain's hissing sound filled the doorway as Mrs. Ringley opened the door. Waiting was a thin, slightly bent-over man of about seventy with a skimpy beard and white overalls. Ben Drumlin the carpenter was keeping an appointment to build shelves in the Ringleys' basement.

"Such a miserable evening," Mrs. Ringley said.

The old man entered and stamped his feet before commenting with a grin: "Rainy weather, dry weather, the nails go in just as straight."

A carpenter who shows up in a downpour, in a good mood and ready to get on with the job, is not a typical carpenter. Ben Drumlin was different in other ways. By day, he ran an antiques shop, where he rebuilt old clocks. Roderick, forgetting his gloom, sat up as he remembered something else. Until Ben's wife died, he had lived in the mountains of New Hampshire — northern New Hampshire, in fact, where people can count on snowy winters.

Roderick rushed back to his dinner. After gulping down his salad, he bounded down the basement steps to ask a life-and-death question:

"Mr. Drumlin, how deep is the snow in New Hampshire right now?"

Taken by surprise as he was making some measurements, the carpenter scratched his partly bald head. "Well now," he said. "Depends which part of New Hampshire you're talking about."

"How about the northern part where *you* lived?"

"Changes from one week to the next."

"True, but how deep do you *think* it is?"

Forced to give a number, Ben Drumlin said, "Two feet. Yes sir, easily that much."

3

Roderick's eyes danced as he gave a long whistle. "Two feet! I bet people can ski right outside their houses from November to April."

The old man nodded. The only trouble, he said as he picked up a long pine board, was that he couldn't take the harsh winters any more. Not even in New Jersey. As soon as he finished a few more carpentry jobs, he would be off to Florida until spring.

"Florida!" Roderick's face twisted into a sneer as he pronounced the name of a state with palm trees. "It never snows at all down there," he said. "Think what people are missing."

Ben Drumlin carefully drew a line for sawing. "Roderick, you seem to have a mighty powerful interest in snow," he said.

"That's because it's like nothing else you can name! Think of it, Mr. Drumlin. Delicate, six-pointed crystals of frozen water, coming down by the billions and turning the whole town into a great big fun-and-adventure party."

Ben went on marking lines as Roderick talked. "From the very beginning," he said, "snow's been the biggest thing in my life. On the evening I was born, my mom and dad say, they barely made it to the hospital through a winter storm. From the time I was six, our family has gone cross-country skiing in Vermont every February. We go up and down some really steep trails at the Trapp Family Lodge in Stowe, with me leading the way."

To get ready for the latest winter, Roderick said, he had gone all-out. Right after the soccer season ended, he had bought books about the weather, polar explorers, and celebrated mountain climbers. At the town library he had read up on the famous blizzard of 1888, when snowdrifts reached second-story windows — "right here in Lysander!" That afternoon, hoping snow would finally come, he had set his cross-country skis by the kitchen door.

The carpenter laid down his pencil. His gray eyes narrowed as he came to a decision.

"Roderick, if you're so taken with snow," he said, "I've got something at my place that you might find interesting. Yes sir, you more than anybody."

When Roderick asked what it was, Ben Drumlin put up a hand. "No time to talk about it now," he said. "If you still feel the same way about snow on Saturday morning, come to my shop. But get there early, before customers show up. This is for your eyes and nobody else's."

Chapter Two

Saturday morning was clear and windy. Happy to skip little-league basketball, Roderick went off on his ten-speed bike after breakfast. He easily found Ben Drumlin's antiques shop, a weather-beaten converted barn on the edge of town.

Entering through a creaky door, Roderick saw nothing at first but old tables, chairs, and what seemed like a hundred ticking clocks. All showed approximately the same time — 9:10.

"So you found the place."

Startled, Roderick noticed Ben Drumlin half-hidden at a workbench in a far corner. He was putting a broken chair back together.

"Did you get these clocks to work, Mr. Drumlin?"

"Every one."

Roderick noticed an even more fascinating object: an old sleigh with faded red paint. "Drove that for years up in New Hampshire," the carpenter said without taking his eyes from his work. "Hitched up my horse and gave people rides to the ski slope. One of these days it'll decorate somebody's lawn."

"That's all a sleigh is good for this year," Roderick said.

"Still feel the same way about snow?"

"Of course!"

"Wait right here."

Ben Drumlin disappeared into a tiny house next to the barn and returned a few minutes later. Dangling from his hand by a drawstring was a worn-looking buckskin pouch the size of a man's fist. Both sides were decorated with beads in a design that looked like a cornstalk. Sticking out the top was a folded piece of paper with smeared pencil writing.

"Watch closely," the old man said. He opened the bag and took a pinch of what looked like fine gray powder. Moving to a window, he blew it into the air. The particles glinted in the sunlight and slowly disappeared.

"That's nothing but dust," Roderick said. "Dust that sparkles."

Ben Drumlin had a way of smiling patiently. Sitting down at his workbench, he told his visitor to pull up a stool. "Roderick," he said almost in a whisper, "that 'dust,' as you call it, is like no dust anybody ever saw. You're the first I've ever told about it, so listen carefully."

Roderick, who usually had trouble letting anyone finish a sentence, listened.

"Years ago, as a boy in New Hampshire," Ben began, "I got to know an Indian named Joe Angry Fox. He was a gentle fellow despite the name, with no family and well up in years. Took me on canoe trips and showed me how to split logs. Later, when he was very sick and about to die, I visited him at his bedside. With trembling hands he gave me this bag. Said it had come down to him from his great-great-grandfather."

"The pouch must be really old," Roderick said.

"Centuries old, you can be sure. Anyway, as Joe lay there close to death he told me things he'd never told anyone. About his ancestors, who belonged to a tribe called the Kittahannocks. They lived in part of what's now New York State."

Roderick said he had never heard of the tribe.

"It was a small one, and Joe claimed he was the last of them. Here's the important part. The Kittahannocks believed that the more it snowed in winter, the taller the corn would grow the following summer."

The old man paused and asked: "You've heard of Indian rainmakers, haven't you?"

"Like those priests down in Arizona who do snake dances?"

Ben Drumlin nodded. "Well, Joe told me his tribe had *snowmakers*. It wasn't easy to make out what he said, because his voice was faint and he was coughing. But here's what I remember. His tribe's priests didn't snake-dance. Instead, Joe told me, they would climb to a sacred place — the highest mountain — on a cold, cloudy winter evening."

"Why?"

"It looked like snow, and they wanted to make sure they got plenty. First they'd do a snow dance. Then the head snowmaker would hold out his cupped hands while an assistant poured in a bit of special powder — an amount that would just about fill a thimble. Roderick, it was the same powder that's in this bag. It has an Indian name, and it means something like 'Clouds-Go-Wild.' Next came an incantation." Ben Drumlin stretched out the pronunciation of this word so that it sounded like three words: "in-can-tation."

"What's an incantation?"

"Solemn words, sung to the Great Spirit. They're written on this piece of paper. Before Joe's time, a member of the tribe translated them into English. When the in-can-tation was over, the head snowmaker would stand with his back to the wind. With all his might, he'd blow the powder up into the low-hanging clouds."

"What happened then?"

"There must have been something magic about the stuff. Whatever the reason, Joe said, they got at least ten inches of snow by morning, and sometimes a lot more."

"That's neat!" Roderick exclaimed, showing his braces. "I mean, like, those Indians had the power to change the weather!" Then his smile faded.

"It's too bad," he said.

"What's too bad?"

"Clouds-Go-Wild wouldn't be any good in Lysander. There aren't any big mountains."

Ben Drumlin leaned back and stroked his skimpy beard. Fastening his eyes on Roderick, he said, "I thought you might want to try it out."

"Me? Where?"

"Oh, some hills near here might be high enough. Of course, if you're not interested..."

"But I am! Only, I was just wondering..." Roderick's voice trailed off.

"What?"

"I don't know how to put this, Mr. Drumlin, and don't take it the wrong way. But how come you kept this powder until now?"

The carpenter smiled his patient smile. "Hardly needed the stuff in New Hampshire," he said. "I could have given it to my grandchildren, but they live in Southern California. No point trying to use it there."

"Forget it," Roderick agreed.

"The pouch is yours if you want it," the old man said.

Roderick took it eagerly. "Careful!" Ben Drumlin warned. "Don't spill any."

As Roderick looked inside the pouch he exclaimed, "There's enough here for a whole bunch of snowstorms!" A sly look came over his face as he asked: "What if somebody blew it all into the clouds at once? Would we get a gigantic blizzard?"

The old man chuckled. "Blizzards can be a problem," he said. "It's better to stick to ordinary snowstorms."

Twitching with excitement, Roderick managed to get in a final question as the shop's first customer entered through the creaky barn door. "What's Clouds-Go-Wild made of?" he asked in a lowered voice. "I mean, if I knew, I could make all I wanted."

"I put the same question to Joe," the old man said in a half-whisper. "But I couldn't hear the answer, and a few minutes later he stopped talking. So the people who know are all gone. You'll have to use the powder carefully, Roderick. Try to make it last a long time."

"Thanks, Mr. Drumlin, thanks a million!"

Roderick pedaled furiously home on his bike. Every few minutes he checked to make sure Clouds-Go-Wild was in his pants pocket. Over and over he said the name aloud and thought: Wait till Brad McCorkle hears about this!

Chapter Three

"A gift from a dying Indian! Last of the Kittahannocks! Roderick, that guy is putting you on!"

Brad McCorkle was not showing the expected enthusiasm.

This wasn't so surprising, Roderick knew. His neighbor and best friend, who was short and stocky with thick red hair, had already decided to study engineering after he finished high school. Practical-minded, that was Brad. An awful lot of what people told him, he believed, was baloney. Including the amazing things Roderick was telling him about Clouds-Go-Wild.

"I'm telling you, the pouch is really old," Roderick said as they walked toward Lysander's main shopping street.

"Sure. Just scatter a little of that wonder dust, say some hocus-pocus, and down comes the snow. Roderick, you're too much." Brad stared at him with his dark eyes.

"Will you just listen! All I said was that Clouds-Go-Wild will make it snow *harder*. Brad, you never listen to anything."

"Look who's talking."

Sooner or later, their conversations wound up like this. Brad would tell Roderick he was "too much," just as he had at the end of the soccer season. That's when Brad had been voted most valuable player on the team, but

Roderick had gone on giving him tips for improving his game.

Roderick realized that his know-it-all attitude could get on people's nerves. But he considered himself a natural-born leader destined to become President of the United States. This meant that he couldn't resist passing out valuable advice. Brad was just as bad. This kid had the idea that *he* was headed for the White House. After a brilliant career, that is, in which he would become the head of a billion-dollar computer company.

"Let's face it," Brad said. "This is the real world, not *The Lord of the Rings*. That old man cooked up a fancy story to get rid of a piece of junk."

For a moment, Roderick wondered if Brad could be right. But then he broke into a smile. "If Mr. Drumlin made it all up," he asked, "how do you explain the incantation on the piece of paper? Are you going to tell me he spent hours writing that? Just to get rid of something he could have tossed in the garbage can?"

Brad's lips curled downward in a frown. Roderick had him this time.

"Well, maybe he's on the level," Brad said, looking straight ahead as he walked. "But I don't see how you can produce a snowstorm with a thimbleful of powder."

"I've checked it out," Roderick told him. "You don't get snowflakes until the moisture in the air, which is picked up from the oceans, condenses around tiny specks of dust to form clouds. The Indians used the special powder for cloud-seeding, just the way aviators do when they drop chemicals from the sky to make rain for the farmers."

"Roderick, come on! You're talking about tons and tons of snow. That would take a miracle." Another stare from Brad's dark eyes.

"Not necessarily." Roderick lowered his voice. "The guys who drop the stuff from airplanes don't use much, either. That's because it's extremely potent. It starts a chain reaction that makes the clouds go to work."

Brad thought about that for a while. "I guess that might be possible," he said, "if the powder worked like a catalyst."

"A what?"

"It's a word from chemistry. It means something concentrated and special. You need only a tiny amount to make something really big happen."

Roderick stopped walking and faced his friend as he said: "Whatever that stuff is, Brad, why don't we try it out? Just the two of us."

You would hardly expect a future engineer to turn down a chance to participate in this kind of experiment. "It's a deal," Brad said. But the whole plan almost collapsed right then and there, when a fellow sixth-grader named Otis Snevily turned up on his bike.

Talk about snobs! His full name was Otis FitzWilliam Snevily III. Behind his back, Roderick called him Otis the Third, the way you'd refer to a king. Brad had been seeing a lot of him lately. With straight blond hair and a California surfer's good looks, Otis the Third was a star player on Roderick's basketball team and a top student. He appeared to be totally aware that he was terrific at everything.

"Too bad you missed the basketball game," he said to Roderick. "We killed the other team."

Brad changed the subject. "Roderick has been telling me some pretty amazing stuff."

What was Brad doing! The last person Roderick wanted in on his secret was Otis the Third.

"What kind of amazing stuff?" Otis asked.

"Well, like, how the weather works and what causes snow."

"Oh." Otis shrugged. "Who cares?" He changed the subject and soon rode off.

"Otis is getting cockier than ever," Brad said.

"I wondered when you would notice."

Three days went by before the weather was right — three very long days for someone as fired-up as Roderick Ringley. Three days that made him realize what a drag the sixth grade was turning out to be. Mrs. Corbett, his teacher, had been giving him a hard time about his sloppy handwriting. A girl named Stacy Zimmermann, who was on Roderick's basketball team, bugged him constantly from her adjoining desk. She and Roderick, both second-stringers, played alternate quarters at the Saturday little-league games. When it wasn't basketball Stacy talked about, it was the Finchley Dancing Classes. What a pain she was!

Maybe, he thought while continuing to wait, he should forget about Ben Drumlin's magic powder. Why not solve the snow problem the best way of all, by moving north? Roderick had read of the glories of living in Buffalo, New York, which receives ninety-five inches of the stuff a year. Moisture from nearby Lake Erie, which meteorologists call "the lake effect," accounts for the heavy snows.

One evening Roderick asked his father for the sixth time, "Why don't we just move to Buffalo?"

"I told you," Dr. Ringley said, puffing on a pipe. "Doctors have to live where their patients are. Besides, we like it in Lysander."

"But just think, ninety-five inches! Three times as much as here!"

"Roderick, you'd get sick of so much snow."

"Oh, you always say something like that!" His son stomped out of the room.

At last, on the third day, Roderick's face brightened as he looked out the window at breakfast. Wispy cirrus clouds high in the sky, sometimes called "mare's tails," were the first sign that a storm might be on the way.

The clouds were the first in a parade that grew lower, thicker, and darker. Roderick knew their names. After cirrus came cirrostratus, followed by altostratus and stratocumulus. Finally came the lowest and darkest cloud layer of all, nimbostratus. Most people would have found it dreary and menacing. But Roderick, gazing at it from Mrs. Corbett's class, was so excited that he got six wrong in a spelling test. When his eyes met Brad's their nervous grins flashed a message: Tonight's the night!

By dinner time the temperature was in the twenties, and Roderick's Snow Watch was back on maximum alert. Once again, he leapt up from the table and rushed to the kitchen phone to get the weather report.

Once again, Dr. Ringley shook his head and said, "That boy doesn't know when to stop."

This time Cora said through her teeth, "I hope it rains cats and dogs." Her father glared at her.

Instead of slamming down the phone as he had before, Roderick squealed with delight when he heard the recorded message: "... a winter storm warning is in effect, with possible snow accumulations of one to three inches."

Excusing himself, Roderick said he was going over to Brad's to work on "a big science assignment." In a way, this was the truth and then some. What could be more scientific than the experiment he and Brad were about to perform? It just didn't involve reading books and doing research. It was 7:15. He promised to be back by 9:00.

Meanwhile, Brad McCorkle told his parents he was going over to Roderick's — also to work on a science project. They met, wearing knapsacks, at a gap in the back fence between their houses.

Heading off to their destination, they soon passed Otis Snevily's big house. The sight of Otis in a bedroom window, bending over his homework, gave Roderick a warm and satisfied feeling. Here he was, on a secret expedition with Brad, and Otis the Third was excluded!

They walked fast, practically jogging, and Brad began to ask detailed questions. This guy never stopped.

"How can we be sure the powder will reach the clouds? Did you ask Mr. Drumlin about that?"

"No," Roderick said. "And it's too late anyway because he's left for

Florida."

"Wouldn't that stuff work better if it were dropped from an airplane?"

"That's not necessary! You know as well as I do, Mr. Engineer, that some air currents swirl upward in storms." As Roderick spoke, they passed under a street lamp. Their breath trailed behind them like little streamers.

Brad had another question. "What about those Indians in New York State? Why did they think the snow would help them grow corn?"

"Simple! It made the soil moist for spring planting. When the heavy snow finally melted, it was like a rainfall postponed until it did the most good."

They were now at the edge of town, where the streets curved steeply upward. The houses were farther apart, with big, dark spaces in between. A half-hour after leaving home, they arrived out of breath at two old stone gateposts. They marked the entrance to Lockridge Hill, the name of a Victorian mansion overlooking Lysander that had been torn down years ago.

A faded "No Trespassing" sign, wrenched loose by vandals, dangled from one gatepost. Beyond stretched a winding driveway covered with weeds and broken bottles, which led to a grassy meadow where the big house had once stood. A raw wind bit at the boys' faces and rustled tall spruce trees that lined the driveway like black sentinels.

The place gave Roderick a creepy feeling. Everyone in town knew that the old mansion had been demolished after a celebrated murder. In recent years, the grounds had become a meeting place for drug addicts and other bad characters.

Roderick wanted to get the snowmaking over with and dash home to watch the results. But once Brad agreed to do something, he wanted to do it right. He was, after all, a future engineer. He liked to talk about building bridges with "a margin of safety" — so strong they can't fall down. When engineers try to "cut corners" by skimping on materials, Brad would say, the bridges collapse.

"Time to put the stuff on," he said.

"This will take forever!"

"Roderick, if those Indians got the results they wanted, it was by putting on a proper Indian ceremony. This is no time to cut corners."

Setting down his knapsack with an angry thump, Roderick pulled out a headband with feathers. It was left over from four years ago, when he and Brad had been Indian Guides. With a bit of adjusting they managed to get the headbands on. Then they smeared their faces with red and black theatrical makeup left over from Halloween.

After several minutes of preparation they examined each other with flashlights. "I hope this satisfies you," said Roderick.

"A little sloppy," said Brad, "but it'll do."

Brad looked as if he were headed off to war. With his streaked face and his red hair sticking out over his headband, he would have terrified a band of Apaches.

They walked past the gateposts and up the long driveway to a great lawn in front of the demolished mansion. Their chosen spot was a forty-foot cliff at the edge of the lawn. A college student had been arrested for trying to hang-glide from there. Since then it had been called "the hang-glider's cliff."

The lights of Lysander and a half-dozen other towns twinkled below. Roderick had learned from a map that the hilltop was 512 feet above sea level, the highest point in the county. It was a pretty puny mountain by Indian standards. But you could almost reach up and touch the nimbostratus clouds, which were getting lower by the minute.

"Let's get on with the snow dance," Roderick said as his teeth chattered.

For the next five minutes, they put on an imitation of the authentic

Indian dancing they had seen at a meeting of their Scout troop. Leaping about flinging their arms wildly, alternatively grinning and scowling in the darkness, they yelled "hey-a, hey-a" until they were hoarse. Luckily for them, no other mortals were around to witness this effort to catch the attention of the Great Spirit.

Now came the incantation. "Are you sure you know it by heart?" Brad asked.

"Of course!" They had practiced saying the incantation dozens of times.

"Let's stand with the wind behind us," Roderick said, "just like we're supposed to." While Brad held a flashlight, Roderick reached into his pants pocket for the buckskin bag decorated with cornstalks. Carefully, using his open parka to shield his hands from the wind, he poured out about a thimbleful of Clouds-Go-Wild.

"Be sure not to spill any," said Brad.

"Don't worry!"

"Ready with the incantation? Remember to sound serious. One, two, three..."

Roderick held out his hand with the powder, closed so tightly that his fingernails were digging into his skin. Together, teeth chattering more than ever, two clumsily costumed figures in feathers and war paint recited words used by tribesmen on much higher hills centuries before:

Spirit of winter wind,
Carry this high
To stir up the snow clouds
And whiten the sky.
Spirit of winter wind,
Work while we sleep.
Bring us a snow blanket

Heavy and deep.

For good luck they said these words not once but three times. That was another "margin of safety" suggested by Brad. Roderick took a deep breath. Quickly opening his hand, he blew with all his might, like someone trying to put out 100 candles at once. It may have been his imagination, but the specks of magic powder seemed to sparkle in the darkness as the wind carried them off.

"Let's get out of here!" said Roderick. They ran down the long driveway as fast as they could, past the line of black trees and the stone gateposts.

Twenty minutes later, with their Indian headbands back in their knapsacks and their war paint hastily removed with Kleenex, they were in front of Brad's house and panting furiously. Just before they parted, Roderick felt a snowflake on his nose, followed by more. "All right!" they yelled as they jumped up and down, playfully punched each other, and ran in circles.

An hour later, an inch had fallen. "Keep on coming!" Roderick said half-aloud as he gazed out the window before going to bed. "Don't quit now."

Chapter Four

Dr. Ringley was awakened before dawn by the scraping of metal on concrete — the sound of Roderick shoveling snow. Roderick always got moving before breakfast when there was snow to be cleared and money to be earned.

But the scraping sounds were thick and muffled. This snow was deep! If Roderick hadn't been so busy, he would have noticed his father peering out a bedroom window in disbelief. The weatherman had blown it again, Dr. Ringley told himself. The bottom panes were nearly covered on the outside with flakes, and the wind was tossing more of them against the glass. Beyond the window, pine and spruce trees looked as if giants had applied huge gobs of vanilla cake icing. Plows had left ridges of snow in the street, and everywhere it was white, white, white.

In the midst of the whiteness was Roderick, happily flinging the snow left and right. More often than he needed to, he rested and let the six-pointed crystals blow right into his face. His green wool cap and chestnut curls were frosted with snow and clammy with perspiration. But that didn't matter. At least a foot had fallen, Roderick figured, and it was still coming down fast.

For years, he had leapt out of bed at a time like this, before his father had a chance to use the family's orange snowblower. But Roderick had another reason to be outside. The winter had at last created a whole new world — his kind of world. He wanted the untouched yard all to himself before others messed it up with footprints.

Once the sidewalk was cleared, Roderick put on the cross-country skis he'd been waiting a year to use. Moving off from the kitchen steps, he had the wonderful sensation of planting the skis in deep, fresh powder, where they sank in far above his ankles. He cut a long diagonal track across the yard as he headed toward the street.

Beyond the yard, a few adventurous folks were up and about. But in the wide streets that Lysander was so proud of, the snowplows had cleared only narrow lanes. Cars had to inch along as their drivers peered through flying flakes that coated windshields between each flick of the wipers. People on foot were dodging the cars. Some were coming back from the station, where the trains had failed to show up.

Roderick felt like a veteran Nordic racer as he swung his arms and glided along on his skis. Here and there he had to slip out of them to cross bare spots left by the plows. That hardly slowed him down at all, because cross-country skis and poles weigh practically nothing. Carrying them quickly to good snow, he'd be gliding along again in seconds. Mounds of piled-up snow were no problem either. Roderick easily scampered up and over them with the skier's "herringbone" step.

It took him ten minutes to cover the seven long blocks from his house to a park near the center of town, where the steeple of a 200-year-old church rose behind a duck pond partly hidden in snow. Continuing on for a few more blocks, Roderick saw men just beginning to clear the sidewalks in front of stores.

Back home by breakfast time, he stumbled into the kitchen, red-faced from all the shoveling and skiing.

His mother had her worried look. "I hope you didn't overdo it," she said.

"Of course not," Roderick panted.

Ski shoes still on, he headed straight for the telephone, leaving a melting white trail. Brad must have been waiting, for he answered after one ring. The conversation was brief.

"Well?" asked Roderick, glancing around to see if the family was listening. This was code language for, "Did Clouds-Go-Wild work or didn't it?"

"*Wow!*" said Brad.

Moments later, the Ringleys got the word that the schools would be closed. Cora let out a big "Yaaaaaaaay!" Roderick grinned, revealing his braces, and soon the grin became wider.

He switched on the radio and heard the familiar voice of Brian Bayne, the weather man on the all-news station:

"... by the time the snowstorm moves on it will have dumped five inches on the New York metropolitan area..."

"Five inches!' Roderick cried. "They ought to fire that guy."

"... there is, however, an exception to this picture. Several counties in New Jersey are really getting buried in snow — more than twelve inches so far. Everything over there is at a standstill."

Roderick practically ripped the phone from the wall as he called Brad again. Meeting out on the street, he and his friend gleefully slapped each other and hurled snowballs. To help celebrate, Brad had brought along a bag of popcorn, which he could never get enough of.

Soon the two were arguing as usual, and Roderick did what he often did. He put his foot in his mouth. "All this snow," he declared with a sweep of his hand, "proves that I was exactly right."

"About what?" Brad wanted to know.

"Clouds-Go-Wild works! I mean, it works so well that we didn't need to bother last night with the headbands and the makeup. Brad, that was just a waste of time."

"Now wait a minute!" his friend said. "It's obvious that an Indian substance won't work without a proper Indian ceremony."

"Oh, brother!" Roderick threw up his hands.

"Admit it, Roderick Ringley. You don't know everything. You'll make a fine Secretary of State when I'm President."

"You've got it backwards. You'll make a fine Secretary of State, Brad McCorkle, when *I'm* President."

They both laughed. After the popcorn was gone, they threw snowballs at the lower twigs of trees, causing them to spring up and release little clouds of flakes. The snow stopped falling, the sun appeared, and everywhere people began digging out from a total accumulation of fourteen inches.

A more serious debate began when Brad had another thought. "Don't get mad when I say this," he said. "It's only a possibility."

"What is?"

"Maybe all this snow is, well, a coincidence. You have to admit, Roderick, we could have had this big storm anyway, without Clouds-Go-Wild."

"Brad, we both heard the radio! It snowed three times as hard here as anywhere else. There's no question we caused all that extra snow. How can you even *think* it's a coincidence?"

"All right! Don't have a spasm."

"Well," Brad said after they had both cooled down, "I guess there's only one way to prove the magic powder really works. Like good scientists, we need to repeat the experiment and see if we get the same results."

"Now you're talking! We've got to produce another big snow."

"But deeper, if possible."

"Right. Why settle for fourteen inches?"

There was no more arguing that day. Shoveling snow together, Roderick and Brad made $13 apiece. Roderick happily added his earnings to a wad of bills in his desk drawer. School was cancelled the next day, too, and Roderick laughed when he heard it. How ridiculous! He was sure that up in Buffalo, where they knew how to handle snow, they wouldn't keep the schools shut for a mere fourteen inches!

Not until the weekend did life return to normal in Lysander, New Jersey. The supermarkets were again fully stocked. All the town's parking lots were cleared. The trains were running on time. But people went on talking about the Big Snow as if they would never forget it. They hoped the winter had no more surprises like this one.

Roderick and Brad had other ideas. Just a week after the snowstorm, wispy white "mare's tails" again appeared high in the sky. During the next twenty-four hours bigger and darker clouds moved in. By the following afternoon the weather report on the telephone was predicting "a possible accumulation of one to two inches."

After a hurried dinner, Roderick was out the door with his knapsack.

"Two lousy inches!" he said to Brad as they met at the fence in the dark. "We can improve on that, just the way the Indians did."

The trip up the hill took a bit longer this time, for they had to bring along skis and poles. They needed them to go from the gateposts at Lockridge Hill to the hang-glider's cliff. Once again, they put on Indian headbands and war paint. Brad insisted on it, as well as an extra five minutes of dancing. "This is no time," he said as he had before, "to cut corners."

In bitter winds, with the temperature in the teens, Roderick and Brad leaped and flung their arms and shouted "hey-a, hey-a" until they were ready to drop. Then, after Roderick carefully poured out a precious bit of Clouds-Go-Wild, they recited the ceremonial words three times:

Spirit of winter wind,
Carry this high

To stir up the snow clouds
And whiten the sky...

Roderick blew even harder this time, and the magic powder disappeared in the low, dark, nimbostratus clouds. He was home at exactly 8:56.

No flakes appeared until shortly before bedtime, when Roderick saw them dancing past the street light. When his alarm went off at 5 o'clock the next morning, he hurried downstairs to the kitchen. To open the storm door, he had to push hard against a wall of fresh snow. He ran for a yardstick and measured the depth at the bottom of the back steps.

Sixteen more inches!

Chapter Five

Dressing with the speed of light, Roderick waded out from the kitchen door. The second storm was beyond his wildest hopes. Drifts were three feet high in places, and he laughed aloud as he stumbled and pushed toward the street light to explore. All around him, tree branches sagged under new snow.

Soon, Dr. Ringley was awakened again by the sound of his son's shovel. When Roderick burst into the kitchen for breakfast, his face was nearly purple from the digging, which was heavier than before. For the second time in ten days the schools were closed, and Cora was again in a festive mood.

Mrs. Ringley looked perplexed. "What is *happening* to our weather?" she asked. But Roderick grinned his widest grin ever when he heard what Brian Bayne, the radio weatherman, had to say:

"Old man winter must have a grudge against some of our suburbs to the west. It looks like the New York metropolitan area will get seven inches of snow, but it's a different story in parts of northern New Jersey. Some places there have been hit with twice as much!"

Roderick practically knocked over his mother as he ran to the telephone to call Brad. They quickly met outside on skis.

"We did it again! We did it again!" Roderick shouted. The snow had stopped falling. But the plows were still at work, and he could barely make himself heard over whining motors and scraping blades. "Brad, now we're absolutely sure that Clouds-Go-Wild is a magic catalyst. We've proved it!"

Brad said he wasn't going to argue this time. But his expression showed doubt.

"What is it?" Roderick asked.

"Nothing."

"Tell me."

"Well, look. Roderick, you must admit, all this snow could *still* be a coincidence. Sometimes the local weather gets stuck in a certain pattern..."

"Aw, come *on*!" Roderick slammed his green cap down on the soft snow.

"To be *really* sure a scientific experiment works," Brad insisted after his friend calmed down, "you have to repeat it, not just once but several times."

They agreed that the only way to settle the matter was to make a third trip up Lockridge Hill.

For the next two days, they helped shovel more snow than they had ever seen in Lysander. This time, Roderick was able to put $22 in his desk drawer. It took three days for life to get back to normal, with the supermarkets once again stocked, the parking lots cleared, and the trains running on time. By then the neighbors were sure the winter had done its worst. After all, the weather records showed that you got two big snowstorms in a row only once or twice in a century.

But while people talked this way, Roderick kept searching the sunny skies for storm clouds. Around the middle of February, they returned. The nimbostratus was practically sliding along the top of Lockridge Hill when Roderick and Brad went off late one afternoon to perform their ceremony in 21-degree cold.

Flakes began to appear before dinner. The third snowfall was gentler, and continued off and on through the night. But by early morning, when the stars finally appeared between fast-moving clouds, another ten inches had come down. Once again — incredibly — the accumulation was heaviest around Lysander.

People were stunned. You got three big snowstorms in a row only once every 200 years or so. What on earth was going on?

Roderick Ringley knew exactly what was going on. And his great enterprise almost came to a halt because he was not very good at keeping his lips zipped.

They began to unzip that evening. The Ringleys invited some neighbors and their kids, most of them weary from digging out, to drop in for a party.

"That settles it!" said a barrel-chested, loud-voiced man who lived down the street. He was standing in the den near Roderick and Brad, who were drinking Cokes while gazing at a crackling fire. The man said he'd been offered a job in Dallas, Texas, and by golly he was going to take it. "Sun belt, here I come!"

"I thought the world was supposed to be getting warmer," said a tense-looking woman with thick glasses. "If you ask me, it looks more like the new Ice Age."

Roderick couldn't stay out of that kind of discussion. The big snows were the greatest thing that ever happened, he said. Besides, he'd heard of an Indian tribe that had a way of making it snow really hard. "Just think," Roderick exclaimed, "how valuable that would be for ski resorts!"

The barrel-chested man had a different opinion. "That would be messing with the weather," he said. "Anybody who tried that around here would belong in jail."

Time to change the subject, Roderick realized in the nick of time.

Just then, those standing around the TV set learned that the big snows were making Lysander famous. The anchorman on the evening news said: "Today the weather played more tricks in northern New Jersey, which is beginning to look like Eskimo-land." The Lysander municipal building, a handsome brick structure close to the village green, appeared on the screen along with a familiar face. It was Elliott Winville, Lysander's mayor, standing by a huge mound of cleared snow with a microphone around his neck.

"This normally peaceful town," a network interviewer beside him said, "has suddenly found itself in the middle of a new snow belt. Tell me, Mayor Winville, how are the citizens of Lysander coping with all this white stuff?"

Elliott Winville was a paunchy man in his mid-fifties with a crew cut and small eyes close together. "I want to take this opportunity," he declared in a resonant voice, "to tell everyone out there how proud I am of the way the people of our fine community are pitching in during this terrible ordeal."

"You tell 'em, Elliott!" said someone by the TV set.

"Sounds like he plans to run for a second term," Dr. Ringley muttered. He was puffing on his pipe.

"But aren't these storms hurting the local economy?" the television interviewer continued.

The mayor looked serious. "No doubt about it," he said. "Stores are losing thousands of dollars. Lysander's factories — we have a few, very clean and nonpolluting — have had to shut down repeatedly."

Roderick barely heard these words. As soon as the mayor was off the screen, he motioned to Brad to follow him upstairs to his bedroom. They shut the door, in case Cora came snooping. "Time to get back to business," Roderick said. He reached to the back of a high closet shelf where he kept the buckskin Indian pouch decorated with beads in the design of a

32

cornstalk. As Brad worked on a bowl of popcorn he had brought up from the party, Roderick carefully emptied the contents of the pouch in little thimble-sized piles on a sheet of newspaper.

"Enough for twelve more snowstorms!" he said, straining to hold his voice to a whisper. "Brad, we can keep the snow going right into April. Why, some years it gets down to the twenties in early May..."

Brad looked worried. "Don't you think all this experimenting has gone far enough, Roderick? Like, isn't it enough to prove that the stuff works? We could get in big trouble. Didn't you hear what that man said about people who mess with the weather?"

Roderick Ringley wasn't ready to stop at all. Did the Wright brothers give up flying just when they'd figured out how to stay airborne? Does a football coach retire when his team is suddenly on a winning streak?

"Why quit now!" he whispered, his blue eyes flashing. "Brad, don't you realize the power we have? We can do what people have talked about for thousands of years. We can change the weather! After we've had our fun, we can turn Clouds-Go-Wild over to science."

"But look at all the inconvenience we're causing," Brad said. "Look what the mayor said."

"Oh, nobody's really suffering. They'll make up all that lost business later on, just the way we'll catch up in school." Roderick changed the subject to a more important matter. The third trip up Lockridge Hill had produced only ten inches of snow. "Something went wrong," he said. "Whatever it was, we need more practice."

"Roderick, I'm telling you. We've already had enough snow." Brad's dark-eyed stare practically drilled through his friend.

"You don't understand!" Roderick said. "With something important, there's no such thing as enough." With the determined expression of a racing-car driver in the final laps of the Indy 500, Roderick added: "We're still way behind the ninety-five inches of snow Buffalo gets. We've got to catch up and pass them!"

Brad tried his strongest argument: "The more times we sneak off, the bigger the chance that we'll be caught."

Roderick fired back with an even stronger argument. "You sound like a nervous old woman," he said.

Brad dropped the subject, at least for now.

Chapter Six

Change the weather!

Beat Buffalo!

These words hardly began to express what snow meant to a kid who had waited and waited for it. Snow was a thousand different pleasures.

Snow was the cushiony stuff you could fall on without getting hurt, as Roderick did for pure pleasure the next morning. Landing on his back, he would lie for minutes on end, watching his breath and squinting in the bright winter sun.

Snow was a symphony of special sounds — icicles dripping, tires spinning, shovels clinking. All that afternoon, people were busy clearing sidewalks, Roderick and Brad included. Normally quiet streets were alive with the shouts of neighbors who rarely met face to face. They complained about the frightful weather, but Roderick noticed that their voices were full of cheer.

Snow was war and peace: giggling snowball battles by day and incredible quiet at sunset. Hardly a car or pedestrian was seen as Roderick and Brad tramped home from the day's shoveling, their pockets full of crumpled bills. Tall, bare oak trees were etched against a cold pink-orange sky, and the smell of log fires promised a lazy evening before the television set. As he stamped his feet in the kitchen, where dinner was steaming away, Roderick was sure of one thing: Right after a new snow, life is as close to perfect as it gets.

But Roderick loved snow for more than the fun it brought. Snow gave him power — power to move around Lysander and power over bullies like Freddy Keezer.

After three big winter storms, most people had to walk carefully between high ridges of snow heaped along streets and sidewalks. Not Roderick Ringley, who could go anywhere on his cross-country skis — through yards, over half-buried fences, across frozen streams. Until the snowstorms hit Lysander, some of Roderick's classmates had laughed at cross-country skis. "Skinny skis," they called them, for sissies afraid of the downhill type.

The laughing had stopped. Heavy downhill skis and their clunky boots, the others now realized, are useless for getting around in a snowbound community. Kids soon begged to borrow Roderick's skis, with their flexible bindings, and the special shoes made for them. The shoes were attached to the skis at the toe, leaving the heel free to rise.

"Downhill skiing is OK," Roderick told the others with a confident air. He could do that stuff too, and had bombed down quite a few slopes. "But cross-country," he said, "is the genuine, original form of skiing. In Scandinavia they've dug up skis 7,000 years old. Whole armies got around on them."

This gave Brad an idea. On the second morning after the latest storm, he invited Roderick and five other sixth-graders who owned cross-country skis to meet at a vacant lot. Three were in Mrs. Corbett's class: a tall stringbean named Chris Tuttle, a mathematics whiz with glasses named Bill Goodbody, and a happy-faced kid named Greg Melnick. The other two, Mike Fontana and Shawn Babbitt, went to a different school.

Brad proposed that they form a "corporation" to perform snow-clearing and delivery jobs. He would be "president" and Roderick would be "chairman of the board." Roderick named it the Scandinavian Ski Troop. "We'll go everywhere on skis," he said, "but with shovels and knapsacks instead of bows and arrows. When we're not working we can go off on long hikes through the snow." The idea was accepted with cheers. Roderick and Brad kept to themselves, however, the secret of the magic powder that made the Ski Troop possible.

When Roderick used snow as a weapon, it was sometimes only to tease. Later that day, Stacy Zimmermann was treated to the "avalanche." Roderick and Bill Goodbody had been given the job of shoveling three feet of accumulated snow off the roof of a neighbor's wrap-around front porch. Then they saw Stacy approaching. She and a friend named Heather Garrity were coming to visit a girl who lived in the house.

As the girls reached the porch steps, a thick shower of snow forced them to stop. But the weather was clear and there was no wind! They saw nothing as Roderick and Bill crouched and tried to keep quiet. When Stacy and Heather moved toward the front door again, a bigger shower of snow sent them running. After the third avalanche, the boys revealed themselves with shrieks of laughter and let the victims through. Stacy was too stuck on Roderick to get angry. "You and your crazy stunts," she said half-jokingly while brushing herself off. "What gets into you?"

Freddy Keezer deserved something nastier: the snow pit. He was an overweight twelve-year-old who lived two blocks from Roderick and Brad and used lots of swear words. Recently he had "borrowed" money twice from Roderick without repaying, and had punched him in the ribs for no reason at all. The kids in the neighborhood were sure that foul-mouthed Freddy, who was repeating the sixth grade, would wind up a bum or a jailbird.

Roderick thought up a way to get revenge, and Brad contributed the kinds of ideas you would expect from a future engineer. Late that afternoon the two hollowed out a large hole in a four-foot-high drift just inside Roderick's front yard. They piled snow around the edges to make the hole deeper; that was one of Brad's little touches. Then they covered it with twigs and newspapers and sprinkled loose snow on top to conceal it.

They hid and waited in a network of tunnels, which they had built since the second snowstorm. Out of an opening in one of the tunnels, only twenty feet from the trap they had prepared, their heads popped up every few minutes looking for Freddy.

At last they saw him coming up the street in his slouching walk, with a cigarette hanging from his mouth. Putting his good baseball-pitching arm to use, Roderick hurled a fast snowball that hit Freddy on the shoulder. The cigarette dropped, and with a frown Freddy picked it up and looked around. Seeing nothing, he walked on. Two heads popped out of the tunnel opening.

"Freddy Keezer is a jerk!" the heads said together. Two more snowballs flew, one hitting Freddy just above his ear.

"Why you little..." The furious Freddy rushed into the snow to punish his attackers. Held up by a layer of crust, he had no idea how deep it was. Then... *thwack*! In he went, almost up to his shoulders. By the time he climbed out, covered with snow and muttering a stream of awful words, Roderick and Brad were gone. They were crawling like a pair of moles, as fast as their hands and knees could take them, through a long tunnel that led to Brad's kitchen door. Once safely inside, they laughed without stopping for five minutes.

When Brad was able to talk, he said: "Did you see the look on his face as he went down!" More laughter. But soon Brad warned, "Freddy will be after us now."

"So what," Roderick said. "Anytime we see him coming, all we have to do is head for deep snow. After today, he'll be afraid to follow us. Look what can happen!" They laughed again.

Roderick was feeling so good about the snow that he proposed a celebration. Mrs. Ringley had a fit when he announced the type of "party" he had in mind: a sleepover with Brad in a snow cave. "You could freeze to death without anyone knowing!" she said.

"Mom, you don't understand," Roderick said. "Snow is an insulating material that helps protect you from the cold. Eskimos perspire in igloos. When fliers crash-land in the Arctic, they build snow caves to keep from freezing while they wait for rescuers. We'll be in winter sleeping bags and take along pemmican in case we get hungry. Can't we, Mom, please!"

"Pemmican?"

"Well, it's not exactly what the polar explorers used, but it's close enough." He held out two sticks of pepperoni, his version of the high-energy food source developed by North American Indians.

Hours later, as the lights went off in the Ringley house, Roderick and Brad relaxed from their heavy work. Scooping here and packing there, they had expanded a section of snow tunnel into a chamber big enough for two sleeping bags. By each boy's head was a snow shelf. On Brad's were a transistor radio, a book on the Big Bang theory of how the universe got started, and a good supply of popcorn. Roderick had a book, crackers, a knife, and his two sticks of pepperoni-pemmican. Remembering every detail of a survival lecture at Scouts, he and Brad had closed off both ends of the cave with bricks made of snow crust to keep out the cold. To create air vents, they had pushed sticks through the roof and left a small opening at the entrance to the chamber.

The temperature in the cave was pretty cold. But Roderick was comfortable enough in his sleeping bag, which he had been careful to place over a pad of plastic foam for extra insulation. He began reading aloud by flashlight about the explorers who raced to the South Pole early in the Twentieth century. A Norwegian expedition had beaten a British group headed by Robert Scott, whose members died later of hunger and cold when they were only eleven miles from where they had stored food.

This bothered Roderick.

"That's so stupid," he said. "They should have kept going."

"Roderick, you're too much!" Brad said. "I'd like to see you after you'd walked hundreds of miles in sub-zero weather and horrible winds."

These details silenced Roderick, but not for long.

"Maybe those people who say the world is getting warmer are wrong after all," he said. "If a new Ice Age comes, nobody will be better prepared for it than us. Brad, guys like you and me will be running everything."

Brad yawned and was soon asleep.

Before long Roderick, too, was asleep. He was dreaming about a place where nearly everything was white and blue — the white of snow and the blue of sky and ice. He was the King of the Snows, sitting on a throne in a great hall with glistening ice pillars. By raising his hand he commanded snowflakes to fall in thick slanting lines as far as the eye could see.

When Brad rolled around noisily in his sleep, Roderick woke up and looked at the luminous dial of his watch. It was 3:30 a.m. Switching on his flashlight, he gazed in wonder at the whiteness surrounding him and his friend.

"Nobody ever had it this good," he whispered to himself. "Nobody!"

But as Roderick was about to discover, his carefree life of fun and adventure was too good to last.

Chapter Seven

Roderick Ringley would have merrily produced snowstorm after snowstorm until all the people in Lysander had gone mad. But before that could happen, he had an unpleasant little encounter with Augustus Gleede. Like an unexpected obstacle that looms in front of a car speeding down a road, Gleede forced the events of that unforgettable winter to veer off in a new direction.

The incident took place just after Roderick and Brad went up Lockridge Hill on a cloudy evening in the last week of February. Snowstorm Number Four came through with twelve inches of dry powder — not bad, Roderick thought, considering that the coldest part of winter was over.

Once again, Brian Bayne reported on the radio that the area around Lysander was hit hardest. This time the President of the United States, no less, came to town by helicopter to have a look. On the evening TV news he appeared with Elliott Winville, who ordered lots of photographs taken for the mayor's next election campaign. Then a face came on the screen that impressed Roderick even more: the mayor of Buffalo! Lysander was having trouble finding places to dump its snow. The leader of a city that gets ninety-five inches a year had come to give advice.

Roderick hoped to keep the town snow-covered until early June. That would give him time to learn karate in case Freddy Keezer gave him any trouble. Outside his bedroom window, in a part of the yard where the sunlight never reached, Roderick planned to build a twenty-foot snowman. With luck, he figured, he might have snow to gaze at — well, maybe a patch of slush — on the Fourth of July.

The prospects seemed glorious — until Augustus Gleede became a major complication in Roderick's plans.

Some grouches you feel sorry for. They want to be nice but for one reason or another — nerves or a bad back — they keep saying mean and insulting things that they later regret. J. Augustus Gleede, whose initial stood for Justinian, was a widower in his sixties who lived in Roderick's neighborhood. He had plenty of money and no serious ailments that anybody knew of. Possibly he was lonely, or he may have been frustrated that he hadn't reached a higher position in the world. Whatever the reason, he was *not* a person who wanted to be nice. In fact, he enjoyed being rude to people the way others enjoy eating a dish of ice cream. For Augustus Gleede, the best treat of all was insulting anyone he considered ignorant or stupid.

In his opinion, that meant practically everybody. Most people, Gleede thought, were "fools, fatheads, and featherbrains." He enjoyed taking advantage of them at Hardwick Hardware, a store he owned. Customers called it Hard-Nosed Hardware because of its high prices. But they kept coming because it was conveniently located next to Lysander's biggest supermarket.

Roderick Ringley had heard that people got ripped off at the hardware store, and that its owner was what his father called "an old curmudgeon." Only recently, Gleede had slammed the door on two kids who had come by his house selling bumper stickers for the soccer league.

In other words, Roderick should have known what he was getting into when he tried to get a job shoveling Gleede's sidewalk.

The morning after he saw the mayor of Buffalo on TV, Roderick set

42

off to earn money with Greg Melnick, the happy-faced member of the Scandinavian Ski Troop. The air smelled deliciously of snow, which clung to twigs and wires in ragged little threads.

"Boy!" Greg said when they looked at Gleede's long sidewalk, which had gone unshoveled all winter. "This could keep us busy until lunch."

If they had known that Gleede was asleep, they would have waited a while to come by. This particular old curmudgeon, a fan of late movies on TV, rarely turned in before 3 a.m.

RRRRRING! RRRRRING!

Greg pushed on the doorbell long and hard, and a dog barked inside. "It's 8:15," he said as Roderick leaned on his snow shovel. "He's got to be up by now." After two more rings, they heard footsteps.

The boys jumped when the door was flung open by a tall, thin, slightly stooped man with bushy eyebrows. His face was nearly purple with anger.

"How dare you disturb people so early in the morning!" Augustus Gleede bellowed. He was in a worn bathrobe. His gray hair was uncombed and his eyebrows quivered. "I'm calling the police right now," he said, and started to close the door.

Roderick had to think fast. "We're, uh, sorry, sir," he said, and asked if Gleede wanted his sidewalk cleared. "We didn't think we'd be disturbing anybody at *this* hour."

Good old Roderick had put his foot in his mouth, and he kept right on doing it. "You're supposed to keep your sidewalk cleared," he said. "It's the law."

Gleede's expression softened into the sarcastic smile he used when dealing with fools, fatheads, and featherbrains. "Young man," he said, "I don't need lessons on the law from someone as ill-informed as you. Besides, as any idiot would have noticed long ago, people don't use the sidewalks in this neighborhood. They walk in the wide streets."

"But they use the sidewalks when the streets are slippery, sir," Roderick persisted. "If they don't they can get run over by skidding cars. *You* could get run over too."

"Highly unlikely," Gleede snapped. "Not that it's your business, but I never go anywhere on foot. Especially not in deep snow."

A glance at the open garage showed why Gleede didn't worry about the condition of his sidewalks. Parked inside was a 1965 Jeep station wagon with four-wheel drive.

"We'll cut our price," Roderick pleaded.

"The answer is no!" Gleede thundered, sounding almost as if he were having fun. He shut the door with a bang.

All that day, Roderick was quiet and moody for the first time in weeks. "Is something wrong?" Dr. Ringley asked after dinner.

"No!" his son shot back, in a way that meant that something was.

Soon Roderick learned that the old curmudgeon did other things besides rip off the customers of Hardwick Hardware and give kids a rough time. At dinner one evening, without revealing his reason, he casually asked what his parents knew about the man who had slammed the door on him and his friend.

Gleede had made most of his money, his father said, from real estate deals. And he usually took unfair advantage of the other party.

At that very moment, Dr. Ringley revealed, Gleede was hoping to pull off the meanest — and most profitable — real estate transaction of his life. Moreover, his chances of making a bundle of money had improved because of all the winter storms.

Roderick was startled by these words but tried not to show it. These were the very same snowstorms, he knew but did not say, that he and Brad McCorkle were creating!

"It's a shame what that man wants to do," Roderick's mother said. Roderick sat up and began peppering his parents with questions about

Gleede's latest deal.

Not far away, Dr. Ringley told him, stood an old farmhouse with a sagging barn on four acres of woods. This was no ordinary four acres. It was the last big piece of vacant land on Stockton Avenue, one of Lysander's busiest streets. Stores, automobile showrooms, and parking lots practically surrounded the property. Gleede planned to buy it, tear down the farmhouse, and sell the land for a taco house and a mini-mall of shops.

"What's wrong with that?" asked Roderick, who liked to eat tacos by the plateful.

For one thing, his mother said, this was no ordinary farmhouse. Records showed that it had been built in 1740 — thirty-six years before the Declaration of Independence — by a settler named Zephaniah Sedgwick.

Roderick knew that Lysander, founded in 1720, was proud of its colonial past. "It is strongly believed," a local historian had told one of his school classes, "that shots were fired in these very streets during the Revolutionary War."

It was bad enough that Gleede wanted to destroy a historical landmark, Roderick's mother said. Even worse was the low price he was going to pay. "He's practically stealing the place," Mrs. Ringley said.

Roderick wanted to know how he could get away with such a thing.

Gleede could be charming when he needed to be, Dr. Ringley explained. Nearly a year ago he had "smooth-talked" the owner into agreeing to sell the whole property for next to nothing. The owner was an elderly spinster named Amelia Higgins, the great-great-great-great-great-great-great granddaughter of Zephaniah Sedgwick. Roderick remembered that in his Cub Scout days he had stopped at the farmhouse several times to sell flowers. Amelia Higgins was hard of hearing, he remembered, but kind of pleasant. She had bought flowers every time.

Miss Higgins, Roderick's mother said, knew nothing about property values. She was financially well-off and wanted to move to a small condominium that would be easier to take care of. Her main concern was having plenty of time to get ready to move, because the farmhouse was crammed with the "paraphernalia" of ten generations of Sedgwicks. So it was easy for Gleede to talk her into giving him a one-year "option" to buy the place for $100,000. That gave her the time she needed, Dr. Ringley said, but "pinned her down" to a low price. The place was worth far more, and the value was rising fast.

"What a chiseler!" Roderick said. "Isn't there a way to stop him?"

Not really, his father said. Amelia Higgins had later found out that $100,000 was a ridiculous sum. But Gleede wouldn't let her out of the "option agreement," which she had signed. The only hope now was that Gleede would not tear down the farmhouse once he became the owner. A group of community leaders wanted it preserved as a museum of life in the 1700s.

"What did Gleede think of that idea?" Roderick asked.

"Featherbrained," Dr. Ringley said, "and he didn't hesitate to tell them so." But the old curmudgeon had finally gone along after the mayor, the president of the town historical society, and the publisher of the *Lysander Weekly Echo,* the local newspaper, put the pressure on. They got him to agree that, on the same day he took over the property from Amelia Higgins, he would turn right around and sell it to an organization that would convert it into a museum. But in return for going along with this plan he wanted prompt payment, and in full. And he insisted on the same price he hoped to get by bulldozing the property for a taco house and mini-mall: $300,000.

"That's an outrage!" Roderick said. "He'll triple his money."

Actually, the property was worth even more by now, Dr. Ringley said. And Roderick did not like what he heard next.

A campaign was under way, his father said, to raise the money needed to buy the property from Gleede. But the bad weather was making it difficult to raise funds. Gleede expected payment by March 12th, when the one-year option agreement was due to expire. That was now barely a week away. And the fund drive, called Save Old Sedgwick or S.O.S., was one-third short of its goal.

"Isn't that bad news for Gleede?" Roderick asked.

"Not at all. He's delighted."

"Why?"

"Don't you see?" Roderick's father said. "If the fund drive fails, Gleede can squirm out of his agreement to sell Old Sedgwick for a museum. If I were in his shoes, I'd be praying for another big snowstorm."

For reasons unknown to his parents, a strange look came over Roderick's face. He, too, wanted another big snowstorm. But how could he enjoy it fully if it was going to help an old curmudgeon like J. Augustus Gleede get his way? For the first time since Ben Drumlin had given him the buckskin pouch containing Clouds-Go-Wild, Roderick Ringley found himself in a ticklish situation.

Minutes later he was over at Brad's, reporting the disturbing new information behind a closed bedroom door.

"We sure don't want to help that guy," Roderick said. His red-haired friend agreed. As far as Brad was concerned, this was one more reason to quit making those trips up Lockridge Hill.

Roderick wasn't ready to go that far. But he said they should put off the next snowmaking ceremony for a week. "That will give those fund-raisers a better chance," he said.

For someone as crazy about snow as Roderick, this was an enormous sacrifice. But soon he changed his mind.

The next days brought mild weather. Birds sang loudly and the sun beat down as the temperature reached the fifties. Snow melted at an alarming rate, and cars made motorboat-like waves as they moved through deep puddles of water and slush. Grownups, out strolling in sweaters, said this was a sign that spring would come early. Surely the town deserved it!

Roderick became anxious and fretful. The roofs of some snow tunnels in his and Brad's yards caved in. Bare spots with spring-green grass — how awful! — appeared on some of his favorite ski trails. Was his whole wonderful white world about to turn liquid and flow down to the sea?

Frantically resuming his Snow Watch at the kitchen telephone, Roderick forgot about the man who had been so rude to him and a fellow Ski Trooper. Soon the weather report on the phone told of "a new storm system, approaching from the southwest." That evening Roderick met Brad, who was walking the McCorkles' Irish setter.

Just as soon as the clouds and the wind were right, Roderick said, they should head for the hang-glider's cliff.

"Roderick, do you know what you're saying!" Brad whispered. People were starting to wonder if the world was coming to an end, he said. A local minister had warned in a sermon that the snowstorms were a form of punishment. And what about old Gleede, who would love to see the fund-raisers' plans ruined by more snow?

None of this bothered Roderick. "Oh, they'll find the money they need," he said. The warm spell must have helped the fund-raising campaign, he added. Besides, look how generously people always gave to Lysander's United Fund and other organizations. Then he turned serious. "We've got to have more snow, Brad, to repair the tunnels. And we're still forty inches behind what Buffalo gets."

"Who *cares* about Buffalo!"

"Let's at least produce enough snow to make up for what melted. How about if we use Clouds-Go-Wild just one more time?"

"No, and this time I really mean it." Brad was tight-lipped as he looked his friend in the eye.

Roderick was sure Brad would change his mind. But all of a sudden, there was more to life than the pure joy of snowmaking. There were things to worry about. And bigger difficulties were about to arise.

Chapter Eight

If there's one thing worse than complications, it's trouble — especially the kind that can get you busted.

The secret of the trips to Lockridge Hill got out.

All along, Roderick had a pretty good idea of who might tell on him, starting with Cora. The little busybody had been serving herself ice cream in the kitchen when he came in from the fourth snowmaking ceremony. Smudges of war paint were plainly visible on his face. Mumbling only a "hi," she had looked him up and down suspiciously and rolled her eyes.

Then there was that snooty so-and-so, Otis F. Snevily III. Roderick and Brad had repeatedly passed his house on the way to the hill. Had Otis seen them, and was he waiting for a chance to reveal what he knew? After all, Otis the Third didn't like being left out of things.

And what about Brad, who could no longer be counted on? Roderick got a good scare the day after their latest meeting, when he noticed Brad talking with Otis on the way home from school. All he could hear was Otis exclaiming, "You're kidding!" and "I don't believe it!" Was Brad shooting his mouth off?

As it turned out, Roderick was wrong about all three. Cora and Otis knew nothing, and before long Brad was again participating in the great snowmaking adventure. That same afternoon, cirrus clouds high in the sky signaled the arrival of the promised storm system. Roderick went to work on Brad. "You can't run out on me now," he said as they met in the snow cave.

His red-haired friend argued and pleaded, but at last he broke into a mischievous smile. "All right," he said. "But I'm doing this strictly in the interest of science."

There was another person Roderick should have worried about and didn't. The one who finally blabbed.

Himself.

In a way, you couldn't blame him. It was not easy to keep your lips sealed when you knew what this kid knew. Not when Lysander had become world-famous for its freakish weather. Not when the President of the United States had come to town, when newspaper reporters and television correspondents kept appearing, when top weather experts were trying to figure out what was causing all the snow — and when Roderick Ringley was sure he knew the answer.

It's even harder to keep a secret when you have a chance to impress somebody.

Roderick would have been furious if anyone had hinted that he wanted to impress Stacy Zimmermann. But lately he had stopped calling her a pain. Shortly after he played his "avalanche" trick on her, he had let her coach him in handwriting. Thanks to Stacy's help, it was becoming possible to read some of his sentences. And he was not blind. He knew that his "teacher," with her warm brown eyes and straight, shoulder-length blond hair, was one of the prettiest girls in Mrs. Corbett's class.

The truth began to leak out when Stacy made an anti-snow remark. She was standing alone with Roderick in a corner of the gym the following day, looking out the window. The succession of clouds that he knew so well had passed through: cirrostratus, altostratus, and stratocumulus. Now, good old nimbostratus was back.

"Here we go again," Stacy said with a sigh. "Another crazy snowstorm."

"Crazy!" Roderick protested. "How can you say such a thing?" After a pause, he looked at her with his head tilted boastfully. In a low voice he asked: "What if I told you the real reason for all the snow we're getting?"

Stacy drew back. "What are you talking about, Roderick?"

"What if I said it's the work of somebody who's able to influence the weather?"

"A person?"

"Yeah!" Roderick said, almost in a whisper. "And what if I said the person was me?"

Stacy stood staring at Roderick. Then she gave him a friendly push on the shoulder and said as she went off: "You and your big imagination!"

If there's one thing more maddening than keeping a secret bottled up inside you, it's sharing it with someone who doesn't believe it. Roderick was now annoyed — annoyed enough to tell more. But he told it to someone quite different than Stacy Zimmermann.

That afternoon, when everyone was standing outside the school building during a fire drill, Roderick bumped into the sweaty, overweight body of Freddy Keezer. "Well, look who it ain't," Freddy said between his teeth. He was still burned up over the snow-pit incident. "Just wait till spring comes, Ringley. I'm gonna get you and that Brad McCorkle. You're both gonna wish you'd never been born."

"I'm not scared of you," Roderick said in a steady voice while feeling weak in the knees. It was time, he decided, to get on with those karate lessons.

"We're going to have lots more snow," Roderick added. "I ought to know, because I can practically guarantee it will happen."

"Guarantee? What're you talkin' about!" the twelve-year-old said. "Nothin's gonna save you, Ringley."

"Oh yeah? I've got the same kind of stuff they drop from airplanes to make the rain come, only it's better. All I have to do is go up Lockridge Hill and poof" — Roderick blew imaginary dust out of his cupped hands — "and we get at least ten inches."

"Sure, and I'm the man in the moon," Freddy said as they returned to their classes.

Freddy wasn't as skeptical as he sounded. You never knew what to believe when some know-it-all kid talked about scientific stuff. So Freddy made a decision. If Roderick were telling the truth, somebody ought to know about it.

That evening, Freddy told his father what Roderick had told him.

A little later that same evening, Roderick and Brad were on their way to Lockridge Hill. As they reached the site of the old mansion and headed for the hang-glider's cliff, a funny feeling came over Roderick that something was wrong. He had done a sloppy job with his war paint. Both he and Brad were tired and went through the snow dance without the usual gusto.

The weather wasn't doing its part, either. Just when Roderick was getting ready to say the incantation and release Clouds-Go-Wild into the sky, the wind stopped. The shivering boys waited fifteen minutes, but the air stayed calm.

"It's getting late, and the clouds are too high anyway," Roderick said with a shrug. "We'll have to try again tomorrow."

They skied down to the stone gateposts. But just as they were getting ready to wipe off their makeup, a waiting police car switched on its headlights. Blinded, the boys heard a policeman step out of the car and say, "You two had better come down to the station house."

Chapter Nine

Two sixth-graders in fierce-looking war paint got stares as they were brought into the police station. A husky uniformed officer with a weather-beaten face led them to a small room furnished only with benches. "You'll have to wait for questioning," he said. "Your parents will be here soon." Before leaving, he gazed at them and shook his head.

Able to talk at last, the two "Indians" burst into an argument that was all the more frantic because of the need to whisper. "I told you this would happen!" said the shorter of the two. "Four snowstorms weren't enough for Roderick Ringley. We had to try for a fifth!"

"Will you just calm down!" said Roderick, who was not too calm himself. "Look, all we have to tell them is that we were skiing on Lockridge Hill and decided to dress up this way for fun."

"Who's going to believe a story like that?" Brad whispered. "They'll think we belong to some weirdo religious cult. Or they'll think it's a cover-up — that we went up there to drink beer or smoke pot." Brad's face took on a grim expression that looked even grimmer under his red hair and makeup. "If we tell lies," he said, "we may be guilty of perjury, which is a criminal offense. You want that on your record for the rest of your life?"

"That could be a problem, all right," Roderick agreed. "But if we tell them everything about the snowmaking, that might land us in jail too.

There may be a law against messing with the weather without a permit."

"I wish you had worried about that a little sooner."

They decided to tell no lies but to reveal no more of the truth than necessary. A few minutes later the door opened.

"Roderick! Oh, my God, what have you been doing?" It was Mrs. Ringley, unprepared for the war paint. As she threw her arms around her son, Dr. Ringley and Brad's parents followed her into the tiny room.

Looking at his son sideways, Dr. Ringley asked almost in a whisper: "What's the point of the, uh, Indian getup?"

"Dad!" said an embarrassed Roderick. "It's a long story."

The policeman with the weather-beaten face escorted the boys and their parents to an office with a desk, an American flag, some filing cabinets, and a row of chairs for visitors. It was after 9 p.m. when a plain-clothes officer of medium height and stocky build entered and introduced himself. He was Sergeant Frank Zaremba, head of the Lysander police department's juvenile bureau.

"I'll try to get this over with as quickly as possible," Sergeant Zaremba said politely as he sat down behind a desk. He had a firm, no-nonsense manner, as if he knew every alibi the most depraved young lawbreaker could think up. It would be a bad idea, Roderick thought to himself, to commit perjury in this room.

"We got a report," the sergeant said, "about some kind of snowmaking effort up on Lockridge Hill." Dr. and Mrs. Ringley looked nervously at each other. "Would you tell us," the officer asked Roderick, "why you two were up there, looking like a pair of Indian warriors, on a night like this?"

"It's easy to explain, sir," Roderick said. "The weather forecast said snow was coming. Brad and I decided to go up and do this Indian ceremony so we'd get a really big amount."

"I see," Sergeant Zaremba said. "And you weren't up there to drink beer or smoke marijuana, I suppose? There's been a lot of that on Lockridge Hill."

"Absolutely not!" Roderick responded, wide-eyed and earnest. Brad eagerly backed up the story when it was his turn. Both sets of parents, who had been leaning forward in their seats, began to relax.

"Well," the sergeant said after a moment's reflection. "I must say, an Indian snowmaking ceremony" — he paused and chuckled — "is a new one on me. I'd be inclined to believe your story except for one thing. What about this?"

Zaremba reached into a desk drawer and pulled out a worn leather pouch containing gray powder, which Roderick had handed over when he and Brad were picked up. Zaremba held the bag rather casually, and Roderick nearly had a spasm worrying that some of the contents might spill.

"If it's not too much trouble, sir," he pleaded, "could you please be careful with that!"

"Why are you so concerned?" the sergeant asked, now looking cold-eyed. He reached in and took a pinch of the powder between his fingers. Both sets of parents looked alarmed. Could it be cocaine?

"It's not what you think it is," Roderick said. "It's something totally different, a special substance called Clouds-Go-Wild. It's potent — I mean, *really* potent. A tribe of Indians discovered it hundreds of years ago. Ben Drumlin, the carpenter and antiques dealer, gave it to me."

The parents exchanged glances again. Brad began shifting his weight nervously in his chair. Roderick had completely lost control of his mouth this time.

"Hmm," the sergeant said. "It sure doesn't look like any drug I'm familiar with. So how does this Clouds-Go-Wild, or whatever its name is, work?"

Roderick went into a breathless explanation: "It's just like cloud-seeding, sir, except that the Indians didn't do it from airplanes because, well, they didn't have any. This was before Columbus, you understand. So they did the next best thing, which was to go to the top of a high hill and blow some of this powder into the clouds and poof!" — Roderick pretended to blow from his cupped hands — "The next morning there were at least ten inches of snow."

Brad's face had a tormented look.

"Just like that?" Sergeant Zaremba asked. "Poof, and they got ten inches?"

"Well, they had to pick the proper hill, of course. And when you use the powder, the clouds and the wind have to be just right. You also have to go through the ceremony carefully, Sergeant Zaremba, step by step..."

Roderick would have gone on, except that the sergeant had begun to laugh uncontrollably. "Extinct Indian tribe!" he said when he finally calmed down. "Clouds-Go-Wild. Poof and you get ten inches of snow. Excuse me folks, but this one is over the top!" He started laughing all over again, and the parents smiled nervously.

Managing to be serious at last, the head of the Lysander police department's juvenile bureau dried his eyes with a piece of Kleenex, leaned forward, and said to the boys:

"In eighteen years of police work, I've heard a lot of stories. But this one really takes the prize." After a pause, Zaremba decided to wind things up. "Clearly, you've done nothing unlawful except for trespassing on the old Lockridge Hill estate," he said. "So listen carefully. Don't let us catch you up there again!"

As the parents and their sons were getting up to leave, Zaremba added jokingly: "Look, guys, don't you think this town has had enough snow? Here, catch!" Picking up the leather pouch by its drawstring, he slung it to Roderick, who had kept looking at it anxiously. Luckily, none of the precious powder was lost.

Later that evening, a newspaper reporter called the Lysander police department to check up on crime activity. "It's been very quiet," said the husky uniformed officer with the weather-beaten face. Almost as an afterthought he added: "Oh, I suppose you could say one unusual thing happened. Something really nutty. We picked up these two kids who claimed they could" — he rolled his eyes — "create snowstorms."

Chapter Ten

You had to hand it to Roderick. When he landed himself in an even worse mess the following day, he did it with style — on national television.

Derek LaFrance — *the* Derek LaFrance of the top-rated afternoon talk show — came to Lysander to interview the mayor and some weather experts about all the snow. A big television crew set up lights and cameras in the town council chamber at the municipal building, which was next to the village green. Scores of local citizens came early to watch.

A few hours before broadcast time, the show's producer had noticed a brief item in a New Jersey newspaper about two local kids who had tried to perform an Indian snowmaking ceremony. He had a brainstorm. Why not include them in the show?

Roderick Ringley was not in the best mood that afternoon. It was exciting, of course, to rush with his family to the municipal building. Here he was, a future President of the United States, about to appear before millions on TV a little sooner than he had planned. But sitting up on the raised speaker's platform next to Brad, perspiring in his blazer and studio makeup under the bright TV lights, Roderick was nervous.

He was still angry, too, at the way Sergeant Zaremba had kidded him the previous evening. And he didn't care much for this Derek LaFrance character, with his fancy-sounding name. The star of the show, well-dressed and in his mid-forties, had curly blond hair and a tan from living in Southern California. Another one of those places with palm trees and warm winters! Waiting for the show to begin, LaFrance strutted around like a grown-up version of Otis F. Snevily III.

The program began calmly enough. Snowy views of Lysander flashed on the screen as LaFrance spoke in a confident baritone voice:

"The North Pole sits at the top of the world — or so we thought until a month ago. Now it seems to have moved thousands of miles south, to the unlikely place from which we are broadcasting today. All over the nation people are asking: What's causing all the snow in Lysander, New Jersey? Could it be that people who worry about the world getting warmer are wrong, and that it's getting colder instead? Is this town's snow siege a taste of what's in store for the rest of us?"

"We have with us today," the host continued, "the mayor of this snow-blanketed community, as well as two eminent meteorologists. We also have two young guests who — this is no joke — don't think Lysander has *enough* snow."

The host first turned to Mayor Elliott Winville, but cut him off after he started to go on and on about how "the people of our town have pitched in again and again during this truly exhausting ordeal." Next he introduced one of the weather experts, whose name was Dr. Emerson W. Tippitt. A short, twitchy man with close-cut gray hair, Tippitt taught meteorology at a college in upstate New York. He had written seven thick books on the weather.

"Tell us, professor," Derek LaFrance said, "what's the reason for all the snow that's been coming down in these parts? Is the earth getting colder?"

You could tell from Tippitt's manner that he didn't think much of television talk shows. His college had persuaded him, against his better judgment, to appear on the program. "The notion that the earth is getting warmer or colder," Tippett said, as if talking to one of his most thick-headed students, "is totally unproved and requires far more research than has been done."

"Maybe so," said the host, "but how do you account for all the white stuff in this town?"

"I will try to put it as simply as I can," Tippitt said with an impatient sigh. "Every five or ten years the northeastern United States gets stuck in a weather pattern that produces two or more big snows following along the same storm track. When that happens, as is the case this year, some communities situated along the storm track — like this one — receive far greater accumulations than others a short distance away."

Derek LaFrance nodded as if he understood every word. "Yes. I see. Now, can you tell us, professor, what the hard-pressed people of Lysander can expect from those thick gray clouds right outside the building where we are talking? What are the odds of still another big snowstorm?"

Tippitt scowled. "My field, sir, is the study of fundamental causes of weather, which vary little over the long run. I did not come here to make a short-term forecast."

"But surely, Dr. Tippitt, you must know enough, with all your expertise, to give us an informed guess. Think of the local citizens, many of them right here in this room, who may be facing another date with the snow shovel."

"Well, if you insist," Tippitt said wearily. "The chances of another big snowstorm in this area, in my opinion, are infinitesimal. Less than one in ten thousand."

Roderick, who had been listening carefully, made a face and whispered to Brad, "This weather expert stinks."

The other one seemed almost as bad. He was Dr. Sven A. Blomquist, a tall man of about forty with heavy horn-rimmed glasses. He had come all the way from his native Sweden to study the recent weather in the Lysander area. The host introduced him as one who "brings the special insights from living not far from the long winter nights and deep snows of Lapland."

Blomquist didn't waste words. Speaking in a singsong, up-and-down accent, he said he agreed "with most of what my respected American colleague says." Roderick slumped in his chair and looked disgusted.

Now Derek LaFrance turned to the boys. "Our remaining guests," he said almost apologetically to his vast, coast-to-coast audience, "have a different slant on all this which is not — ha ha! — widely shared. I'd like to ask Roderick Ringley, a sixth-grader from right here in Lysander, to tell us about his solution to the snow problem, which is to create more."

Roderick gulped, cleared his throat, and proudly repeated everything he had said to Sergeant Zaremba. As he told how the Indians had blown the magic powder into the clouds — poof! — and had gotten at least ten inches of snow, Derek LaFrance kept nodding his head. "Yes, I see," he said over and over.

"Well, folks," he declared when Roderick was finished, "I guess childhood fantasy lives on in our scientific age!" Laughter rippled through the council chamber. When it died down, Derek LaFrance looked closely at the young guest. "Tell us, Roderick, do you have other magic tricks? Toads for giving your friends warts? A voodoo doll collection?" More laughter.

That did it. For fifteen full seconds, Roderick said nothing. But he could feel his anger surging and his face flushing under all the makeup. Here was this slick television star with his three-piece designer suit, making fun of his story and tossing in extra insults. Besides, he was from a place even worse than Florida — a place where people bragged about getting snow only once every half-century.

Then it all came out. As millions watched on live TV, Roderick blurted into his clip-on microphone: "You just brought me here for laughs, didn't you! Well, Mr. LaFrance, I think you're pretty darned silly yourself."

"Hey, just a minute, young man..."

Roderick couldn't stop now. "If you think Clouds-Go-Wild is a joke," he said with his mouth trembling, "just listen to this." Then and there, he revealed what he had failed to tell Sergeant Zaremba at the police station: "Brad and I have already made it work four times!"

"Four times," Derek LaFrance repeated with no expression.

"Yes! We're the real reason for Lysander's big snowstorms! We went up to Lockridge Hill and did our ceremony with Clouds-Go-Wild, and it worked four times."

At these words, Brad covered his face with his hands.

At last, the words sank in. "Did you say *four times*," the host asked, no longer talking smoothly.

"Yes, we did it!" Roderick said. "We made it work, again and again."

"But, er, uh, today's newspaper story gave the impression that you were on your first trip up the hill. Didn't you tell the police about the other trips?"

"They didn't ask! And they wouldn't have believed us anyway."

"But, well, if what you're saying is true, you and your friend ... uh, could have changed the weather."

"Absolutely!" The camera zoomed in on Roderick as he continued, his blue eyes flashing. "The writer Mark Twain said everybody talks about the weather and nobody does anything about it. Well, we proved that it can be done! All it took each time was a tiny bit of Clouds-Go-Wild. That's the real reason why we've had more snow than anywhere else, Mr. LaFrance. And I'm glad we did what we did, because snow is beautiful and exciting and fun, and I wish the winter would last until July!"

Pandemonium swept through the council chamber, as it does in a courtroom when a witness has blown a case sky-high. But there was no judge with the authority to rap his gavel for silence. Frantically, the show's staff members tried to shush scores of Lysander's citizens, who had begun talking noisily. Many were pointing in anger at the boy who had just spoken.

Up on the speaker's platform, Derek LaFrance kept smiling as he tried to think of what to say.

"Well, well, well!" he exclaimed. "Isn't this remarkable!"

At last his smooth manner returned and the room quieted down as he said: "Since we have two weather experts sitting right here, let's ask them if these boys could somehow have modified the weather. What's your opinion, Dr. Tippitt?"

Tippitt had been listening to Roderick with growing annoyance. "If you will forgive me," he said, trying to control himself, "I refuse to be drawn into answering such a question. The very idea that two boys could change the weather by chanting Indian rhymes and scattering a bit of useless dust into the air is pure poppycock!"

"You mean," the host said, "that this area would have received unusually heavy accumulations of snow anyway?"

"The heavy accumulations," Tippitt snapped, "were a coincidence and nothing more." As he said this, Roderick had a look that said, "This guy is hopeless."

The host turned to the Swedish meteorologist. "What's your view of this, Dr. Blomquist? Do you agree with Dr. Tippitt?"

Nobody was prepared for the answer.

"Actually, I do not entirely agree."

"You, uh, don't?"

"The fact is," the Swedish expert said in his singsong up-and-down accent, "the large amount of snow *could* be the result of people trying to influence the weather."

Not a sound was heard in the council chamber. Derek LaFrance was tongue-tied. Roderick Ringley swung his chair and took a closer look at the professor from across the Atlantic. In some ways Dr. Blomquist looked old for his age: stooped, paunchy, and bald on top. But he tried to make up for this by letting his remaining hair hang down in long curls and by wearing a colorful necktie. He looked to Roderick like someone who gave a lot of A's.

"But, uh, Professor Blomquist," the host resumed, "surely you don't believe..."

Dr. Blomquist then went into a technical explanation. Roderick, straining to listen, found his Swedish accent hard to follow. In addition to his singsong voice, Dr. Blomquist had trouble pronouncing the letters W and J. For "we" he said "ve," and for "just" he said "yoost."

"To this day ve scientists do not fully understand," the professor said with a twinkle in his eye, "the process by which tiny little drops of water in the clouds turn into different kinds of snowflakes. Ve do know that if you seed the clouds with *yoost* the right material — pellets of dry ice, let us say, or silver iodide crystals — you can get what ve call a chain reaction. Suddenly, you can get tremendous amounts of rain or snow."

"Therefore" — he paused for breath — "ve must not laugh at the possibility that these boys could have, shall ve say, modified the weather. It is only a small possibility, of course. And only if the wind was blowing *yoost* the right way to carry the powder up into the clouds, and the powder was *yoost* the right kind."

Silence again. Looking more confused than ever, Derek LaFrance said: "But I still don't understand, Professor Blomquist, how one thimbleful of a 'magic powder' could cause ten inches of snow — millions of tons of it — covering several counties."

"I only said it was a *small* possibility," the Swede reminded his interviewer. "Don't forget," he added with a smile, "the Indians of North and South America have long had many amazing drugs and other substances.

And chemists sometimes get gigantic reactions by using a catalyst."

"Uh, would you explain that to our audience?"

"A catalyst is something concentrated and powerful. Sometimes you need only a tiny amount to make something very, very big happen."

At the mention of this word, Brad, the future engineer, shot an I-told-you-so look at Roderick.

"Well, well!" said Derek LaFrance. "Nothing like a bit of controversy. Perhaps the experts ought to have a look at this magic stuff. How about it, Roderick, old pal? Did you bring it along?"

"No, sir!" said Roderick. "I'm keeping it in a safe place."

By now, Dr. Tippitt looked as if he were ready to blow his stack. "If I may say so," he said, "this afternoon I have seen television sink to a new low. To give publicity to these boys' foolish claims is wildly irresponsible."

"Not so, Dr. Tippitt, not so!" said Dr. Blomquist, who could not let this go by. "The possibility that these boys could have influenced the weather cannot be ruled out. A true scientist should not be dogmatic about these things."

Tippitt leaped from his chair. "Who are you calling dogmatic, you boneheaded Swede!" he yelled. "What are you, anyway, some kind of hippie? Why don't you go back where you belong?"

The gentle-mannered Dr. Blomquist had a hurt look as he singsonged: "I do not think, Dr. Tippitt, that science is helped by personal remarks of this kind."

"Well, we've certainly had a lively program today in Lysander, New Jersey — ha ha! — and I want to thank all our guests." Derek LaFrance spoke at machine-gun speed as the show ended ahead of schedule and the network filled in with taped material. The two professors, waving arms and shouting at each other, looked as if they might get into a fist fight. Policemen quickly led them out by separate doors.

Without saying a word, but looking as if he were ready to boil, Brad quickly left the town council chamber with his family. Roderick now had to face his own parents. "I was going to tell you the whole story!" he whispered as Dr. and Mrs. Ringley came up to the platform. "Honest I was!"

"It's too late for that kind of talk," Roderick's father said, trying to keep his voice down. "You've been lying to us for weeks, and you've disgraced your family!"

On the tense drive home, Cora asked Roderick repeatedly how he could have done such a thing as sneak off to Lockridge Hill time after time. All her brother could say was, "Shut up, will you!"

It seemed as if matters could get no worse. But as the car reached his street, Roderick was dumbfounded by what he saw. In front of the house an angry, arm-waving crowd was gathering. People were chanting, "No more snow! No more snow!"

Dr. Ringley didn't know whether to drive on or put the car into reverse.

Chapter Eleven

"We want that boy!" several voices shouted.

"Just a minute, just a minute," Dr. Ringley pleaded as he climbed out of the car, which he had maneuvered past all the people and the heaps of old snow along the driveway. It was better to go home and deal with the crowd, he had decided, than to cruise around and wait for it to go away. At least 150 people were noisily milling about and waving fists, and more were showing up every minute. Roderick had seen this kind of crowd only once before: in a western movie with a lynch-mob scene.

As soon as Mrs. Ringley and Cora slipped into the house, a human wall closed around the car. Roderick got out and darted to his father's side.

"Can I have a word, please!" Dr. Ringley said. "This is all a misunderstanding."

Dr. Ringley repeated his plea several times, but the chanting of "No more snow!" continued. The human wall — mostly men with arms folded, eyeing Roderick — stood firm. After several minutes, a beefy man of about thirty-five in an oil-stained parka elbowed his way to the car.

"We want justice!" he shouted, and the other voices began to die down. "We all heard your kid on that television show, and that weather expert, Dr. What's-his-name from Sweden. From what he says, that cloud-seeding stuff may really work. And this boy ought to be punished for fooling around with it."

"Yeah!" several people said. "Don't let him get away with it."

A thin woman in her early fifties spoke up. "Roderick Ringley is a menace to society," she said in a shrill voice. "He and his friend have themselves a good time on Lockridge Hill, and the next day the rest of us get heart attacks from shoveling snow!"

Despite his father's protective arm over his shoulder, Roderick was stiff with fear. He stared at the ground to avoid the hostile faces and thought: "That lucky Brad!" No crowd had gathered at the McCorkle house, where his friend was safely inside.

From the corner of his eye Roderick noticed that the clouds were lower and darker. In his ears he could feel that the wind had finally picked up a bit. Scared as he was, he couldn't help wondering: Was Snowstorm Number Five still a possibility? He'd get no help on this one, he was sure. He remembered Brad's disgusted expression at the television show, a sign that his friend was through with magic powder and incantations. If there were to be another storm, Roderick would have to go to the hang-glider's cliff alone. In a town now stirred up against him, this would be risky.

After his father spoke, the chances of getting there looked even slimmer.

"Look, folks," Dr. Ringley said. "I have no idea whether my son changed the weather around here. But let me be clear about one thing. Roderick won't be going to Lockridge Hill any more. In fact, for a long time he won't be allowed to go *anywhere* after dark. And his mother and I have another punishment in mind that will make him very sorry about what he did. Now, does that satisfy you?"

"No, it doesn't!" a fortyish man in the rear of the crowd shot back. "They say there's a 90% chance of snow tonight. If that Clouds-Go-Wild stuff is as powerful as your kid says, there's only one thing to do. The police should keep him in custody until the weather clears."

Dozens of voices roared, "Right! Lock him up!" The chanting of "No more snow!" resumed.

Roderick's stomach churned and his teeth chattered. Then a new threat appeared: Sergeant Zaremba, arriving in an unmarked police car, was moving toward him through the crowd. Roderick figured he was really in for it now.

"Please, folks, please!" Zaremba said after he had worked his way up to where Roderick and his father stood. Two more police cars, marked and with flashing red beacons, had pulled up. Their eerie red light was streaking across trees, houses, and faces.

After the crowd quieted down, the head of the Lysander police department's juvenile bureau introduced himself and spoke in a voice that was both loud and calm: "I know why you people are here. I saw the same TV show you did. But I'd like you all to go home. I'm convinced that this boy, from one of the most respected families in town, hasn't done anything wrong. From the way some people are talking, you'd think he's been practicing witchcraft up on that hill."

"Well, maybe he *has* been practicing witchcraft," a woman's voice said. "Yeah, how about that?" added a man standing nearby.

"Just a second!" Sergeant Zaremba said, trying to sound good-natured. "This is America, folks, and you need proof. There's no real evidence that Roderick Ringley and his friend had a thing to do with the weather."

The street was now silent, except for the squawk of police-car radios. Even little kids, who had been chasing each other on the fringe of the crowd, were listening. "I'll let you people in on something," Zaremba said. "When they brought Roderick and his friend into the police station last night, all decorated with feathers and Indian war paint, I listened to their story. And you know what? I cracked up. I never laughed so hard in my life. I thought the whole thing was ridiculous, and I *still* think it's ridiculous."

A few people started grinning, and some began to leave. But just then a nervous-looking, bald-headed man in his fifties with steel-rimmed glasses came forward and asked for the chance to speak. He identified himself as Vernon Stubbs, owner of the *Lysander Weekly Echo*. He said he was also serving as publicity director and treasurer of the Save Old Sedgwick committee, "which faces a serious emergency affecting the future of this town."

Stubbs talked in a distinct voice that carried far. "I came here because we are using every opportunity to ask for people's help," he said. Because of the terrible weather, he explained, the campaign to save the old Sedgwick farmhouse had run into serious difficulty. A historic building dating from 1740 — more than three decades before the Declaration of Independence — was in danger of being torn down for a taco house. With little more than a day left, Stubbs said, the fund drive to save the landmark was still $30,000 short of its goal.

Roderick looked surprised when he heard this.

"The next twenty-four hours are critical," Stubbs said in winding up his appeal. "Please contribute whatever you can when the fund-raisers call. Give while there's still time."

The crowd applauded lightly, and people were again leaving when someone loudly asked Stubbs: "What about this Ringley kid? If it weren't for him, you might have all your money by now."

"Yeah," said another voice. "What if his cloud-seeding stuff really works? Just to be on the safe side, he ought to be kept out of circulation until you reach your goal." Shouts of "Lock him up!" were heard all over again.

"Well, er, really," Stubbs said, looking somewhat embarrassed. "I don't see how this boy's silly activities could have anything to do with the snow..."

Roderick relaxed, but not for long.

"...but on the other hand, I'm shocked that a pair of boys would even *want* to inflict so much inconvenience on this town."

Silence, except for the squawking police radios. Eyes more hostile than before gazed at Roderick Ringley. You could practically taste the tension in the air.

"That's not fair!"

It was Roderick, speaking for the first time since he had stepped out of the car. "You don't understand!" he said to the newspaper publisher, loudly enough that all could hear. "I was sure that Save Old Sedgwick had collected enough money by now. My dad says that in this town, money for things like that always turns up."

"That's been the case until now," Stubbs said, a quick smile passing over his face. "But not this time, young man! And if we don't get the money soon, Old Sedgwick will disappear, just so one of the richest people in town can become even richer."

"How much money could he make?" Roderick wanted to know.

"Up to half a million dollars."

"Did you say half a million?"

"I certainly did," Stubbs said. "With property values skyrocketing, that's how big a profit Augustus Gleede could get." He explained that a fast-food chain named Tac-O-Rama, which built big sombrero-shaped restaurants outlined in red neon lights, was interested in paying a very high price for the site. "If the citizens of this town don't come up with the money by tomorrow," Stubbs warned, "people may soon be munching tacos on the paved-over site of a colonial farm."

"I've heard enough!" shouted the beefy man in the oil-stained parka. "This kid is cuckoo, and right now he shouldn't be on the loose." The shouts of "Lock him up!" resumed and grew louder. "Take that Indian powder away from him, too," said the woman in her fifties who was worried about heart attacks.

Things were getting out of hand. "Roderick," Sergeant Zaremba said quietly, "you'd better give me the pouch."

"I can't!" Roderick said. "I don't have it with me."

"Perhaps your son should come with us for a few hours, until things quiet down," the sergeant said to Dr. Ringley. "There's no telling what some of these people might do."

"The officer is right, Roderick," Dr. Ringley said. "Roderick? *Roderick, where are you going?*"

Like a slithering snake, his son disappeared down a nearby hole in the snow before anyone could grab him.

"Catch him! Catch him!" several voices yelled, but it was too late. People searched all around the Ringleys' yard, but saw only a barren snowscape with thickly crusted drifts.

"He's somewhere under all that snow," Dr. Ringley confided to Sergeant Zaremba, "in one of the tunnels he and his friend have scooped out."

"Yes, Dr. Ringley, but where?" the sergeant asked frantically.

"I don't know! The tunnels run every which way. He'll have to come up before long. He's not dressed to stay out in the cold, and he'll get hungry."

It was almost dark. After a half-hour went by and Roderick didn't appear, people drifted away. The police stayed behind and waited, and Mrs. Ringley and Cora came out with flashlights to help watch for any sign of movement in the snow.

By dinnertime the police left too. Dr. Ringley promised to call them as soon as Roderick turned up, and went inside with Mrs. Ringley and Cora.

"Mom! Dad!" Cora yelled from the kitchen. "Come here, quick!"

The doors of the kitchen cabinets hung open, and half the bread and crackers was gone. Cheese, baloney, and soft drinks had disappeared from the refrigerator. Rushing upstairs, Mrs. Ringley found Roderick's blazer, spotted with melted snow and mud, hastily thrown on the bed near his good shoes. Returning to the kitchen, she noticed that his parka — and his cross-country skis, poles, and shoes — was gone.

"I don't believe this!" Mrs. Ringley said. "He must have rushed in the kitchen door when nobody was looking."

"He could have changed and grabbed food in five minutes," Cora said.

"Do you suppose," Mrs. Ringley asked in a halting voice, "he has the Indian powder too?"

"It's certainly possible," Dr. Ringley said with a worried look as he went to the telephone to notify the police. "He could be anywhere by now — with enough food for several days."

Chapter Twelve

Up and down the streets of Lysander, cars crawled along as their drivers peered through open windows into the bitter-cold darkness. With powerful flashlights they searched behind bushes, tree trunks, and snowbanks. "There he goes!" the driver of one car called to another car. "Let's get him!"

The hunt was on for Roderick Ringley. But finding him was not going to be easy. He could go on his skinny skis where others couldn't — through yards, over half-buried fences, across frozen streams. To foil pursuers, he moved on top of the deepest snow. The crust would support him, but a grownup who tried to follow on foot would sink in.

Where was Roderick going, the pursuers wondered, and why? Was he so frightened by the crowd at his house that he was running away? Or was he heading for Lockridge Hill to unleash another storm on a snow-weary town?

One of the searchers was Dr. Ringley. As he turned a corner, he noticed something moving. It was Roderick, dashing across the street with his skis in one hand and his poles in the other. He was in a neighborhood on the opposite side of town from Lockridge Hill. Where could he be going?

Flooring the accelerator and then slamming on the brakes near a snowdrift, the fugitive's father called in a loud voice:

"Roderick, I know you're out there. Your mother and I want you to come home! We promise we won't punish you."

Silence.

"Do you hear me, Roderick? Everything is forgiven if you'll come home now. Roderick, we love you."

More silence. Moments later, from behind a distant clump of shrubs, Dr. Ringley heard a familiar voice. "Dad," Roderick called. "I can't come now. I've got important reasons. Tell Mom I'm OK."

"Roderick! How can you do this to us? Roderick? *Roderick!*" Dr. Ringley's son was gone.

Sergeant Zaremba, also looking for Roderick, had a new reason for finding him. The head of the Lysander police department's juvenile bureau had begun to take the Indian powder seriously. On the TV news that evening, Zaremba had seen an interview with a meteorologist in the Midwest. The expert was asked to comment on what Dr. Blomquist had said about Clouds-Go-Wild. Instead of dismissing the stuff as useless dust, the meteorologist said he would give anything to have a look at it.

But as Zaremba soon learned, Roderick had lost interest in the scientific possibilities.

Zaremba stopped his car when he saw fresh ski tracks. Leaping out with bullhorn in hand, he spoke in the direction they went: "Roderick, it's me, Sergeant Zaremba. I've got something important to tell you."

After a pause, a familiar voice said, "Like, what?"

"Well, an important scientist is really excited about the Indian powder. He wants to analyze it to see what it's made of. Roderick, this could make you famous."

Another pause. "I don't care."

"Roderick, give us a break. Stop this nonsense and come out of there."

"I can't," said a voice that sounded farther away.

Roderick covered another ten blocks before he was spotted by pursuers of a different kind. They, too, had been watching television. Their car pulled up where they had just seen Roderick rushing across the street.

A man called out in a low, scratchy voice: "Roderick Ringley. Can you hear me? We want to do some business with you."

Roderick moved closer to the car on his skis. He stayed 20 feet away in deep snow in case the occupants tried anything funny. "What kind of business?" he asked warily.

"We're from, uh, a company," the same voice said. "One that runs ski resorts. We want to buy that Indian powder from you."

"Why?"

"If we could figure out how to make more, it would be worth millions."

Long pause. "Thanks, but I'm not interested in selling," Roderick said.

"We'll pay a lot."

Another pause. "How much?"

"See for yourself." A small leather satchel landed at Roderick's feet. Opening it and switching on his flashlight, he saw that it was full of $5 bills.

"There's $5,000 in there."

Roderick aimed his flashlight for the first time at the man who was talking. He didn't look like a businessman. Appearing to be in his late twenties, he wore a padded winter vest over a wool shirt. His face was thin, and one side of his mouth curled down in a funny way. Next to him, at the wheel, was a pudgy man who seemed to need a shave.

"Keep your money," Roderick said. He tossed back the satchel and quickly disappeared.

"Wait, you fool!" the man with the thin face called. "Come on," he said to the driver. "Let's find him. It looks like we'll have to use force."

Somehow, Roderick avoided getting caught by all those who were after him. Ten minutes after his talk with the "businessman," he arrived at an address he had hastily looked up before leaving home. Removing his skis, he ran to a well-lit front porch to ring the bell.

"You!" said the person who opened the door.

"I need to talk," Roderick said. "It's urgent."

Chapter Thirteen

"I ought to call the police right now! Do you realize they've called the state troopers?"

Vernon Stubbs, the nervous owner of the *Lysander Weekly Echo*, was jumpier than usual — and not pleased to see Roderick Ringley. But after the visitor begged for a chance to talk, Stubbs put on an overcoat and told his wife he was going for "a stroll." The stroll took him close to a bush in his large front yard, where Roderick had put his skis back on in case he needed to make a fast escape.

"I need to tell you about my plan," Roderick said. He moved deeper into the shadows to stay hidden from passing cars.

"Young man, I don't know what's on your mind, but you'd better talk fast. And I'm telling you right now: I'm going to the telephone in exactly five minutes. Your parents must be frantic."

Roderick had trouble getting started. "It's like this, Mr. Stubbs. I've been thinking a lot since I saw that crowd in front of my house. And, like — Mr. Stubbs, I've decided that it's time to give up snowmaking."

Stubbs tapped his foot impatiently. "I see. Well, that's fine. If that's all you came here to tell me, I'll go in right now and …"

"Please!" Roderick said. "I'm not putting this very well. What I mean is, I'm going to give up snowmaking — but not until I've used Clouds-Go-

83

Wild one more time."

"Until you *what?*"

"I've got to do the Indian ceremony, Mr. Stubbs, but not for the reason you think. I want to help you and all the other people on the Save Old Sedgwick committee. And you have a big part in my plan."

"You want to help us! Of all the strange..."

"I know what you must be thinking. To you I'm just an irresponsible, selfish kid who's only interested in having fun. But that's not my reason at all, Mr. Stubbs. This afternoon in front of my house, I realized how much trouble my friend Brad and I have caused everybody. Especially the fund-raisers."

"Oh, you needn't feel so guilty," Stubbs said. "Nobody has proved the bad weather is your fault."

"What really made up my mind was what you said about the old farmhouse. I didn't realize Mr. Gleede has a chance to make half a million dollars on the place. We can't let that guy make so much money, Mr. Stubbs!"

"Well, it may happen."

"But it mustn't! And that's why we need one more snowstorm."

Stubbs tried to calm himself. "Roderick, the last thing on earth we need, with one day left to raise the rest of the money to save a 1740 farmhouse, is another ten to fifteen inches of snow."

"Oh, I'm not thinking of ten or fifteen inches," Roderick said calmly.

"Thank heaven for that."

"Oh, no. I'm thinking of a real blizzard this time. In a situation like this, Mr. Stubbs, you go for broke. I've decided to use up all the Indian powder I have left."

"A blizzard!"

"I figured it out. In the time that's left, a real blizzard is the only way to stop Mr. Gleede."

Stubbs sighed. "How, may I ask, would it do that?"

"Simple." Roderick told what he'd heard from his father about Gleede's "option" agreement to buy Amelia Higgins's property. "Is it true," he asked, "that Gleede doesn't actually own the old farmhouse yet?"

"That's correct," Stubbs said impatiently, not sure where all this was leading. "All Gleede has is a contract giving him the right to buy the place for $100,000."

"But an article I saw in the *Echo* says that the contract runs out at midnight tomorrow. Is that right?"

Stubbs nodded. "Miss Higgins wanted a whole year to get ready to move out, and Gleede was in no hurry once he got her to agree in writing to a ridiculously low price. Besides, that way his money stays in the bank and earns interest right up to the day he pays her."

"Just what I hoped!" Roderick exclaimed. "That means that all we need is a huge amount of snow — a really *tremendous* amount. That way, nothing on wheels will be able to move, not even Mr. Gleede's Jeep station wagon with four-wheel drive. Just think, he won't be able to drive over and pay Miss Higgins by midnight. The contract will run out, and he'll miss the chance to sell to a fast-food chain and make all that money."

Stubbs was dumbfounded. "Roderick, I've never heard of such a far-fetched scheme in all my life," he said. "Why, even if that Indian powder works, which I don't believe for a second, it won't stop Gleede. If it's snowing when he wakes up tomorrow, he'll drive over and pay Miss Higgins early in the day to make sure he doesn't miss his deadline."

"Ah," said Roderick. "That's where you and your Save Old Sedgwick friends come in."

"I'd like to know how."

"Just use the snow as an excuse to stall him! Isn't it true that he agreed to turn around and sell the property to your organization for a museum if you can pay him $300,000 by tomorrow?"

"Well, yes, but he's been hoping all along that we won't come up with the money. If we don't, he can wiggle out of the agreement."

"So, just tell him early in the day that you've *almost* raised the $300,000. Then, make him a proposal that he'll like: If he'll just wait a few hours, you'll bring him the $300,000 you've raised before he has to go and pay $100,000 to Miss Higgins."

"What if he agrees? What happens then?"

"Easy. As the day goes on, keep telling him you need more time to collect the rest of the money. Use the weather as an excuse. Then, if everything works out as I hope, the snow will keep falling and it will get too deep for him to drive to Miss Higgins's house. Midnight will come, and his deal will be dead!"

"Roderick, that sounds... well, dishonest. You're asking us to trick Mr. Gleede into missing his deadline."

"He deserves it after the way he took advantage of Miss Higgins! Besides, maybe you really *will* need extra time, Mr. Stubbs. In that case, you'll be telling him the truth."

Stubbs's head was swimming. "I just don't know what to say about this, Roderick," he said. Something else bothered him. "If the snow gets so deep that nothing on wheels can move," he asked, "how will we be able to move around town to raise the rest of the money?"

"You've forgotten about skis, Mr. Stubbs! The wheels may stop, but fund-raisers on skis can keep on going. I'll send some of my friends to help out. If there's a blizzard, the people they call on will be snowbound in their homes, right next to their wallets, purses, and checkbooks."

The owner of the *Lysander Weekly Echo* shook his head in disbelief. How could fund-raisers on skis gather enough money? He kept looking for other flaws in Roderick's plan.

"What's to stop Gleede from walking through the snow to pay Miss

Higgins?" he asked.

"Are you kidding? Even in perfect weather, he never goes anywhere on foot."

Stubbs thought of another, even more serious, possibility: "What if we don't reach our $300,000 goal and he still manages, somehow or other, to drive to Miss Higgins's before midnight?"

A grin came over Roderick's face. "There's a third part to my plan, Mr. Stubbs, but I don't have time to tell you about it now."

"Roderick, think what you are doing! If you blow all that powder into the sky, it will be lost to science."

"After tonight, Mr. Stubbs, I don't want anybody to use Clouds-Go-Wild ever again. That man in the crowd was right. People have no business fooling around with the weather. And there's more to it than that. I'm starting to see things differently. It's partly because..."

Roderick's voice broke, almost as if he were blinking back tears. "Darn it, well, all of a sudden..."

"What, Roderick?"

"Mr. Stubbs, I think I've had enough snow!"

Not knowing Roderick well, the owner of the *Echo* did not appreciate the full meaning of what he had just heard. A kid who got carried away by things had said the word "enough."

"Suddenly," Roderick continued, "I'm ready for springtime and leaves on the trees. Later on I want to feel the good hot summer sun and go to the beach. I miss the wonderful smell of grass after it's been cut, and the sound of crickets. Thunderstorms are pretty great too. For a long time, Mr. Stubbs, I hoped a new Ice Age was coming. But now, you know what? I don't *care* any more."

But there was no time to talk further about the joys of summer. "I can't stay any longer," Roderick said as he began to push off on his skis.

Stubbs still had misgivings about Roderick's plan. "If the powder works as you hope," he said, "think of all the trouble a blizzard will cause." He had to raise his voice as Roderick crossed into a neighbor's yard.

"Oh, that's no problem. The snow will melt quickly this time of the year."

"Roderick, I'm just not sure about this plan of yours."

"Remember, stall Gleede tomorrow." Roderick's voice grew fainter. "Stall him as long as you can."

Roderick had no time to lose. Within minutes, he knew, Stubbs would be on the telephone. He would tell his parents and the police of his plan to produce a blizzard — but not the reason why, he hoped. Before long, the searchers would all head for Lockridge Hill. He had to get to the hang-glider's cliff before they could stop him!

He knew he had to avoid the stone gateposts, where a police car was sure to be waiting. Instead, he planned to use a nearby trail the Scandinavian Ski Troop had made through the woods on one of its hikes. But as he ran across the road to where the trail started, clutching his skis and poles, he was caught in the light of an approaching car. The car skidded to a halt and a voice said: "Quick, before the others get here!" It was the "businessman" with the scratchy voice.

Putting on his skis, Roderick started to move off into the woods. But the other "businessman," using a flashlight, ran after him on the hard-packed ski track, which supported a grownup's weight. With one of his powerful hands he grabbed Roderick by an arm. "Get that powder, that's all I want!" his partner shouted. Trying to shake free, Roderick reached into his pocket with his free hand for the beaded Indian pouch and held it as far away as he could.

Within seconds, he would have been forced to surrender the precious catalyst. But he suddenly realized that others were present in the woods. He saw the flashing red light of a police car, which had just pulled up. And ahead of him in the darkness a flashlight went on and a voice called: "Over here, Roderick. Throw it!"

❇ ❇ ❇

Chapter Fourteen

The voice behind the flashlight was Brad's.

This was no time to ask why he had turned up on Lockridge Hill. With one arm tugged at by his pursuer, Roderick slung the bag with his free hand in the direction of the flashlight.

"Got it!" Brad said. The man immediately let go of Roderick and plunged into the snow in the direction of the other boy's voice. But Brad had left the narrow, hard-packed ski track for the deep drifts. His pursuer, the pudgy "businessman," sank in to his waist and could hardly move. Meanwhile, his thinner partner was moving toward Roderick, hoping to hold him hostage until Brad gave up the pouch. Roderick, however, had also left the path. Soon the other man was also floundering in deep snow.

Moving awkwardly and waving their arms for balance, the two "businessmen" now found themselves in the glare of other flashlights. Heavy-duty police flashlights. "We'll help you out in a minute," said Sergeant Zaremba, who had pulled up in a second police car. "First we have to get hold of that crazy Ringley kid." Zaremba started to run down the ski track, but suddenly swung around and aimed his light back at the thin man, whose loose lip curled down on one side. "Hey, wait a minute. You look kind of familiar to me. Could it be... We've been looking for you for weeks!"

"Let's forget the kids for now," Zaremba shouted to the policemen from the other car. "We've got bigger fish to catch right here. Come out of there, both of you, with your hands up." The two bigger fish struggled out of the deep snow at gunpoint. They were escorted to one of the police cars and locked in back. Several precious minutes were lost before Zaremba resumed trying to catch Roderick, who was already deep in the woods with Brad.

The two stayed away from the track and moved as fast as they could. Brad had correctly guessed that Roderick would try to get to the hang-glider's cliff, but by a different route than usual. As they approached its base, they paused for a few seconds to catch their breath.

"What took you (puff) so long?" Brad asked. "I waited up here (puff) a whole hour in the freezing cold."

"I had to (puff) see somebody important on the other side of town. But why did you (puff) come? Now they'll be after you too."

"I couldn't resist," Brad said. "What we're doing (puff) is absolutely nuts. Still, I knew (puff) you'd need help."

"Well, thanks. But we'd better keep moving." With many more puffs — and an occasional "ouch" as an unseen twig hit his face — Roderick told Brad of his plan to keep Augustus Gleede from making a profit of half a million dollars.

"Roderick Ringley," Brad said, "I sure hope (puff) you know what you're doing. Because if you don't (puff), we could be fugitives for the rest of our lives."

Quickly removing their skis at the bottom of the hang-glider's cliff, they climbed forty feet of rocks that were mostly bare of snow. The cliff was not as steep or slippery as they had feared. Here and there they could grab hold of small trees.

At the top they found the same breathtaking view that had greeted them on the first snowmaking trip: the lights of Lysander and half the county twinkling below. The clouds were still overhead, thick as ever. You could practically touch the snowflakes that would soon form around billions of invisible drops of moisture in the air. A very special kind of dust, available to only two people in the whole world, would help make it happen.

"We'll have to skip the headbands and the makeup," Roderick said. "There's no time for the ceremonial snowmaking dance, either."

"Roderick, that's what made the powder work before! We mustn't cut corners."

"But Brad, the cops will be here soon. In this kind of situation, I'm sure the Great Spirit will understand."

So Roderick went ahead and cupped his hands. Brad poured out all the powder left in the Indian pouch.

They were about to recite the incantation when they heard a voice.

"Roderick!" called Sergeant Zaremba, who had come by the upper path, approaching as close as he could on the nearest packed snow. "Stop what you're doing! That powder is valuable to science! I'm appealing to you not to use it."

"Don't pay any attention," Roderick whispered. "Are you ready? One, two..."

"Brad! Roderick! Don't do it!" Sergeant Zaremba shouted. "Think of the harm a blizzard could do."

"...three!" As fast as they could, but with extra feeling to make up for it, they recited three times the words of a vanished Indian tribe:

Spirit of winter wind,
Carry this high
To stir up the snow clouds
And whiten the sky.
Spirit of winter wind,
Work while we sleep.

Bring us a snow blanket
Heavy and deep.

Sergeant Zaremba was pushing his way through the deep snow as Roderick took a long breath. He blew harder than he would ever blow again as long as he lived. This time, he and Brad were sure they could see the magic dust — many times what they had used before —shimmer in the darkness as the wind whisked it away.

"Well, I guess it's goodbye forever to Clouds-Go-Wild," Roderick said without any regrets. To emphasize that the snowmaking ceremonies were over, Brad hurled the empty pouch as far as he could into the woods below. Before they fled, Roderick called out to the Great Spirit: "Oh, please bring us a blizzard! For the good of Lysander!"

Slipping and scratching knees in their haste, they climbed down to the bottom of the cliff. Back on skis, they pushed off to a hiding place where they had decided to spend the night.

The town-wide hunt resumed, but the searchers gave up when Mrs. Ringley received a message a few minutes after midnight. Her son, calling from a pay phone, said he had little time to talk: "Mom, I'm warmly dressed, and I've had enough to eat. Brad and I can't come home tonight. Later on we'll tell you why." Click.

By now, four inches of new, white snow covered Lysander's streets. An eerie thought occurred to Dr. Ringley just before he turned in. Gazing out the window with his arm on Mrs. Ringley's shoulder, he asked: "Do you realize what day this is?"

The new day that had just begun, he told her, was March 12th, the anniversary of the great Blizzard of 1888.

❄ ❄ ❄

Chapter Fifteen

Fate has a way of putting bumps in the path of brilliant plans, even those of a strong-willed eleven-year-old who thinks he's destined to occupy the White House. After a promising start, Snowstorm Number Five decided to lie down on the job. The temperature rose during the night, and the snow turned to rain for a while. By morning only seven soggy new inches had accumulated.

Brian Bayne, the radio weatherman, still had plenty to talk about:

"Has a weather mystery in the western suburbs been solved at last? A New Jersey sixth-grader tells the nation on TV that he has been experimenting with an incredibly potent material for seeding clouds. Then he and a friend defy the police and release more of the stuff. The result? Twice as much snow as anywhere else in the region. The whole thing is enough to blow this forecaster's mind!"

It was anyone's guess, though, where the two snowmakers were.

If Amelia Higgins hadn't been hard of hearing, and if she hadn't been busy straightening up, she might have been the first to discover them. Out in the woods, about 150 feet from her old farmhouse, Roderick and Brad had passed the night in a hastily dug snow cave. Roderick wanted a "base of operations" right on the Sedgwick property, in case Gleede showed up to pay his money and the "third part" of his plan became necessary.

"Seven lousy, wet inches!" Brad said after they awoke that morning and peeked out of the cave. Only a few flakes were coming down. They were the big, sticky kind that falls when the weather is about to clear up.

Brad wondered why the huge dose of Clouds-Go-Wild had produced such a small result. Was the Great Spirit angry at them for wasting the magic powder?

"Look, it's still snowing, isn't it?" Roderick said while breakfasting on crackers and Coke.

"That's one way of looking at it," his red-haired friend said, reaching for some cheese popcorn. "But let's face it. Seven inches is worse than no snow at all. It's enough to slow down the fund-raisers but not enough to keep old Gleede from going anywhere he wants to in his Jeep station wagon."

"There's hope," Roderick insisted, "as long as the snow keeps falling. But Mr. Stubbs will have to tell Gleede something pretty convincing to stall him. Meanwhile, we've got plenty to do."

After breakfast, Brad began digging tunnels that might come in handy later on. At the risk of getting caught by the police, Roderick skied over to Bill Goodbody's.

Waiting in some shrubs until Bill came out to shovel, Roderick told him to round up the other Ski Troopers and go help the S.O.S. committee collect money. "If you find anyone else with skis who can ring doorbells," Roderick said, "make him a new member." After dinner, the Ski Troopers were all to join Roderick and Brad at their secret headquarters, where they would be asked to help in a different way.

"How?" Bill asked. "And where's the headquarters?"

"There's no time to talk now," Roderick answered as he dug his ski poles into the ground to leave. "Just be sure to bring the others to the entrance of Crestview Cemetery at 7 p.m. when it's good and dark, and I'll escort you from there. Make sure everybody comes with a snow shovel."

A half-hour later, Bill and the other Ski Troopers appeared at the office of the *Lysander Weekly Echo.*

"Well, well," Vernon Stubbs said with a nervous smile, "our young friend has sent help, just as he promised." The Save Old Sedgwick committee needed all the fund-raisers it could get, he said. Dozens of checks had arrived in the morning mail, but the campaign to save the old farmhouse was still $18,000 short of its goal on the final day. Unless enough money turned up very soon, Stubbs reminded the Ski Troopers, a historic landmark would be replaced by a taco house — "a sombrero-shaped, neon-lit, architectural monstrosity of a taco house!"

By mid-morning, while Roderick and Brad were busily tunneling through Amelia Higgins's yard, their pals were collecting checks.

Stubbs sent the Ski Troopers to the most out-of-the-way homes, many located at the top of steep, winding streets. That made sense, because their residents were more likely to be snowbound and rich. And who could say no to a kid who had taken the trouble to come by on a day like this?

Certainly not people like Brian O'Meara, who lived in a big house with a three-car garage in a high-priced section called Eaglehurst. He was the dashingly handsome head of the town's biggest real estate firm, whose salespersons always told househunters about Lysander's past. "It is strongly believed," the salespersons said, quoting the local historian, "that shots were fired in these very streets during the Revolutionary War." That meant, of course, that homes in Lysander were worth something extra.

Mike Fontana was splotched with soggy snowflakes and out of breath from climbing O'Meara's driveway on skis, when the owner opened the door. "We're making an (puff) emergency second appeal," said Mike, "for funds to (puff) preserve the Sedgwick Mansion..."

"Anything to save our colonial heritage from the fast-buck artists!" O'Meara said. He'd already given once but took only thirty seconds to write and tear off a $500 check.

Many other checks were collected that day. Four big ones were brought in by a new recruit to the Ski Troop: Otis FitzWilliam Snevily III.

Otis's family was high on the list for the emergency appeal. Answering the doorbell when Chris Tuttle rang, Otis the Third practically begged to join the young fund-raisers. "I know a lot of the families on your list," he said enthusiastically, without actually sounding conceited. "You won't be sorry." Chris, who was surprised to hear Otis pleading for anything, lent him an old set of skis, poles, and shoes.

Some of the regular S.O.S. fund-raisers — those who had cross-country skis — also rang doorbells that day. Leading them was a blond, glowingly healthy woman in her mid-forties named Sophie Hopwood. A fitness fanatic who liked to jog in Roderick's neighborhood, she was the high-powered president of the Save Old Sedgwick committee, head of the Lysander Historical Society, and a member of five other organizations dedicated to improving the town. When the going was rough, as it was now, she used athletic expressions. "We'll all have to run harder," she would say in a bubbly, low-pitched voice while flashing a broad smile that showed her perfect teeth.

On the final day of the fund drive, Sophie Hopwood was out on her cross-country skis and wearing a stylish blue and green windbreaker. She concentrated on making calls to leading merchants and other big shots. She also fired up the other fund-raisers, including the new helpers from the Scandinavian Ski Troop. "This time, boys," she told them with one of her biggest smiles, "we'll really have to sprint all the way to the finish line."

As the day wore on, the fund-raisers kept moving and delivered more checks to Vernon Stubbs's office.

One person not on the move was J. Augustus Gleede.

"I don't get it," Brad said in the late afternoon, when perhaps another inch of wet snow had slowly accumulated. "Gleede can easily drive over here to Miss Higgins's, pay his money, and become the owner of the place.

But he hasn't even tried. Are you sure he has to come here?"

"Absolutely," Roderick said. "Miss Higgins can't go to *him* on a day like this. And it takes two to complete a deal."

"Then why is he waiting when his time is running out?"

"I don't know. But it could be something the Save Old Sedgwick committee told him."

"If so," Brad said, "let's hope they keep giving him reasons to wait. The snow sure isn't going to stop him."

Brad was wrong. Fate was about to pull another surprise.

The storm that had been over Lysander since the night before — the puny one that had disappointed Roderick and Brad — was moving slowly out to sea. But before it left the area it was jarred back to life by a new weather system arriving from the north. The re-energized storm became a huge machine for taking moisture from the nearby Atlantic Ocean and turning it into snow.

And so much snow! Within half an hour the gray light of late afternoon temporarily grew brighter, not from the sun but from a blinding curtain of fine white flakes. The flakes did not fall; they *flew* as a northeast wind gathered force and flung them sideways. They flew into yards, quickly filling in cleared paths and forming big new drifts. They flew against the corners of roofs, swirling upwards in little white columns resembling ghosts. And at Amelia Higgins's place they flew against the face of a sixth-grader who danced and waved his arms.

"I knew it would happen! I knew it would happen!" Roderick shouted to Brad, his voice nearly drowned by the howling wind that bent over pines and spruces. "That wind is gusting to thirty miles an hour. Brad, we're getting the blizzard we wanted — it just took a little longer!"

Shortly before 7 p.m., when Roderick left for Crestview Cemetery to meet the other Ski Troopers, another six inches had come down — three inches an hour! As Roderick made his way against the wind, his skis were completely swallowed by powdery drifts. His joy was so great that he didn't even mind seeing Otis F. Snevily III in the group shivering and waiting with snow shovels at the cemetery entrance. Even Otis the Third was welcome now!

After leading the other Ski Troopers to the Higgins place, Roderick disclosed to them his plan to stop Augustus Gleede from making a profit of half a million dollars. He repeated what he had said on the Derek LaFrance show: that Clouds-Go-Wild was the cause of this storm and all the earlier ones. Today the magic catalyst was coming through in grand style. "When you use a lot," Roderick said as if he had known it all along, "there must be a delayed-action effect."

"Speaking of delayed action," he continued, "the S.O.S. folks must have said something pretty amazing to keep Gleede from coming over here." If he tried to come now, Roderick said, the snow was already deep enough to give him trouble. But in case it didn't stop him, it would be necessary to build "a defense line."

They all began moving snow with shovels, piling and packing it to form a wall across the driveway a short distance inside Miss Higgins's property. Earlier, a plow had cleared the long, sloping driveway. Sam Gilstrap, Miss Higgins's lawyer, had just come by in his car to be on hand if Gleede showed up. As far as Roderick Ringley was concerned, Gilstrap's motor vehicle would be the last to reach Miss Higgins's house that night.

By 9:00 the temperature had dropped sharply, and another seven inches of snow had fallen. Plows were unable to keep up with the blizzard. No cars were moving on Stockton Avenue, not even a Jeep station wagon. Had Roderick succeeded at last in stopping all the wheels in Lysander? Maybe, but he soon received unwelcome news.

Greg Melnick, the happy-faced kid, had been sent to spy on Gleede's house. He didn't look so happy after he skied back to the snow cave.

"Gleede's getting ready to drive off," Greg said, and Freddy Keezer and another kid named Jimmy Dolan were shoveling his driveway. "I saw them come by and ask for the job."

"If he's giving the job to guys like that," Roderick said, "he must *really* be worried about getting out."

The work on the "defenses" was stepped up, and two Ski Troopers were sent back to keep an eye on Gleede.

Shortly after 10:00, when the deadline on the "option" agreement was less than two hours away, Greg Melnick reported that Gleede had finally left his house. Twenty minutes later Chris Tuttle, who was keeping a lookout on the town's main shopping street, arrived with further news.

"I just saw a Jeep station wagon pull into the parking lot behind the bank on Maple Street," Chris said. "There were two men, not one, and one of them had bushy eyebrows."

"That's Gleede, all right," Roderick said. "How was the Jeep making it through the snow?"

"Sliding around, even with four-wheel drive, but it got there. When Gleede got out, he kept telling the other guy to hurry. And boy, he did not look happy!"

Chapter Sixteen

After the double-header snowstorm dumped an incredible twenty-four inches on Lysander, the skies cleared to reveal a gleaming three-quarter moon. The raging winds died down. Scarcely a sound was heard anywhere, except the scratch of snowplows or the shouts of a few brave souls out on foot. The town had never seemed more peaceful than it did at 10:30 on the night of March 12th.

Peaceful was not the right word, however, for J. Augustus Gleede. He was frantically waiting to get into the bank on Maple Street. Roderick had been right in thinking it would take a "pretty amazing" story to stall the old curmudgeon. Later he would find out that members of the Save Old Sedgwick committee had telephoned Gleede several times that day. But he would also learn, to his great surprise, that the story they kept telling him was basically true.

That morning Vernon Stubbs, the S.O.S. committee's treasurer, had been the first to call up Gleede. The fund-raisers, Stubbs had told him, expected to reach their goal by the close of the business day, at 5 p.m. Then they would promptly bring Gleede a check for $300,000.

So Gleede had decided to stay home and wait. He still thought the committee's plan to turn the old farmhouse into a museum was "the most featherbrained idea anybody ever cooked up." The property was worth twice as much to the Tac-O-Rama fast-food chain, he knew. But he'd been having trouble reaching those folks, and he had to keep his promise to give the S.O.S. crowd a chance to buy the place. They were a bunch of silly do-gooders, to be sure. But it was also true that if they raised their money he could collect $300,000 in cold cash from them that very day, without any hassle, before he had to pay a penny to Amelia Higgins. He was sure he'd have plenty of time to get to her house. That morning, the snow hadn't seemed a problem for the owner of a Jeep station wagon with four-wheel drive.

Later, at 4:30 that afternoon, Gleede had received another phone call, this time from Sophie Hopwood. The president of the S.O.S. committee sounded full of her usual enthusiasm. The fund-raisers were "within $6,000 of the finish line, Mr. Gleede!" she had said in her bubbly low-pitched voice. And she had "sensational news." She had just learned that a new contributor was prepared to make "an extremely large gift."

There was just one problem, Sophie Hopwood had told Gleede. It would take a while before the contributor could turn the gift over to the fund-raisers. But if Gleede would wait until 10:00, the S.O.S. committee would be able to raise its offer for the property to $350,000.

Again, Gleede had decided to sit tight. How could he pass up an extra $50,000?

But after five more hours had gone by, and the blizzard had done its work, Gleede's face had turned purple with anger. Sophie Hopwood had called at 9:55 to request "just an hour more, because of the *unbelievable* difficulties caused by all the snow."

By now the owner of Hardwick Hardware had had enough from this woman, whom he considered the most featherbrained of the S.O.S. bunch. "I know what you people are up to," he growled. "All day you've been stringing me along! You don't have the money to build that cockamamie museum of yours and you never will. But out of pure spite, you want to trick me out of getting the Higgins place!"

He had decided to leave for the old farmhouse at once. But when he telephoned Amelia Higgins to say he was on the way, he got a surprise. The elderly spinster said he would have to pay her with a special kind of check certified by the bank. Gleede hadn't bothered to get one because he thought a regular check would be acceptable. Did she realize, he asked, the extra trouble she was putting him to? He would have to ask the bank's manager, as a special favor to a big customer, to open up the bank after it had closed. And he'd have to drive with the manager to the bank "on a night like this."

No wonder, then, that Gleede was furious by the time Chris Tuttle spotted him and the manager at the bank's rear entrance. Gleede knew that Amelia Higgins had wised up to the low price in the "option" agreement. In the final hours, he was sure, she was trying to delay him until after midnight. He now had only 90 minutes left to buy her property at a giveaway price.

It was nearly 11:00 when Gleede walked out of the bank with a certified check for $100,000. He was ready to drive the manager home as fast as he could in the deep snow, and pick up his lawyer for the trip to the old farmhouse. But then he ran into another difficulty. A big garbage truck with a snowplow blade, which had been clearing the parking lot, was blocking the exit.

"What's the meaning of this!" Gleede shouted through the side window of the Jeep.

"There's no need to get so steamed up about it, mister," said the driver of the garbage truck. "Can I help it if the engine quits on me?"

The bank manager had a suggestion: "You could always walk to Miss Higgins's place."

"I never go anywhere on foot!" Gleede roared. "And it should be obvious to anybody that the worst time to walk is right after a blizzard."

By now Chris Tuttle was back at the parking lot, out of sight but close enough to hear what was going on. More impatient than ever, Gleede went back into the bank with the manager to make a phone call. Fifteen minutes later, to Chris's surprise, five boys showed up with snow shovels and began removing a huge heap of snow in front of the disabled garbage truck.

"Who are they?" Roderick asked when Chris brought this news back to the Ski Troopers' headquarters.

"You're not going to like this. Freddy Keezer, Jimmy Dolan, and three others who are just as rough looking."

Skiing back to the bank, Chris found Gleede puffing nervously on a cigar while Freddy Keezer's pals shoveled. As the snow flew, so did the swear words. And what sloppy workers! They seemed to be throwing as much snow at each other as they threw to the side.

Several times the group seemed on the verge of fighting. "Watch where you swing that, meathead!" one kid would shout. "Just who are you callin' meathead?" another would snarl.

Gleede, who was paying twice the usual rate for snow shoveling, kept glancing at his watch. "Can't you work any faster?" he asked the group. It took them ten minutes to carve out a passage big enough for the Jeep to get around the stalled garbage truck.

Midnight — and the deadline on the "option" agreement — was now only forty minutes away. Having been stopped once by the snow, Gleede didn't want to be stopped again. As he was getting ready to drive off, he told Freddy and Jimmy to ride along in the back seat with their shovels. The others, he said, were to walk over to Miss Higgins's place on Stockton Avenue as fast as they could — "in case we need help getting up the driveway." For the extra work, he said, he would pay them at three times the usual rate. The Jeep swerved and its wheels flung snow as Gleede drove off with the bank manager, Freddy, and Jimmy.

When Chris brought this information back to headquarters, Roderick,

Brad, and Bill Goodbody looked at each other nervously. Brad was more worried than the others. "Roderick, you told me last night we'd use the snow to stop Gleede," he said. "How are we going to stop Gleede plus five tough twelve-year-olds?"

"No problem at all," Roderick said, though his voice didn't sound very confident. "We'll just have to work extra hard to get ready for them." Then he had another thought. "When they get here, we'd better hide for a while. If Freddy sees us too soon there could be, uh, complications."

For the next ten minutes, Amelia Higgins's place was like a fortress preparing for a siege. Inside the house, only a few lights were on. Amelia Higgins and her lawyer, Ed Gilstrap, were watching a TV show while they waited for Gleede to arrive. The volume was turned up high so she could hear, and they were unaware of the activity outside. Roderick hadn't dared to let the spinster in on his plan, because she might misunderstand and call the police. And that would spoil everything.

Removing snow here, packing and piling it higher there, the Ski Troopers kept working until one of them, Shawn Babbitt, caught sight of the Jeep swerving and sliding in the distance. "They're coming!" he shouted, forgetting to keep his voice down. By now, Gleede had taken the bank manager home and had picked up his own lawyer, who was named Lester Ellis. In back of the Jeep were Freddy and Jimmy with their shovels.

Roderick looked at his watch. It was 11:40. If only they could delay Gleede for twenty minutes! That was all it would take to deprive him of a chance to make a pile of money.

As Roderick, Brad, and the others disappeared into the cave and the tunnels, Gleede turned his Jeep into Amelia Higgins's long, sloping driveway. But just inside he saw a barrier of packed snow looming in front of his windshield and slammed on the brakes. In the last ten minutes the Ski Troopers had raised the wall another foot, to five feet.

Gleede's bushy eyebrows rose. "Somebody's up to dirty tricks!" he muttered. Lester Ellis, Gleede's lawyer, pondered what to do. "Maybe we can get out and climb over the thing," he said. "Or you can stay here while I, as your attorney, hand her the check and sign the papers."

"Stay here? Never!" Gleede wasn't going to miss the pleasure of handing the check to Amelia Higgins. Not after the way she had tried to delay him.

Turning to Freddy and Jimmy on the back seat, Gleede shouted, "Quick! Get rid of that wall!" As the boys started working, their three pals arrived and joined in. Once again, the snow and the swear words flew.

"Stand clear!" Gleede shouted through the side window a few minutes later. After backing the Jeep down the driveway, he threw it into forward. He floored the accelerator and rammed into the two feet of hard-packed snow that remained. *Flump!* The snow stopped the vehicle, whose four wheels spun uselessly. Poking his head through a hole 200 feet away, Roderick grabbed Brad's arm and giggled.

The giggling stopped after the Jeep got through on a second try. It was 11:45, and Amelia Higgins's front porch was a mere 300 feet or so up the driveway. Turning to Lester Ellis, Gleede said: "We've made it! I can't wait to see the expression on the old girl's face!"

He quickly paid Freddy and his pals, who started to walk home. Putting the motor in gear, he easily drove through the nine inches of snow that had fallen since the driveway was plowed. Through his windshield he saw the porch — and the real-estate deal of his life — get closer and closer. Abruptly, though, the driveway became bumpier and seemed to climb steeply. Gleede had to step on the gas. "Funny," he said, "there seems to be a little rise..."

THWACK!

The terrifying sound of cracking branches echoed through the moonlit woods. With a bump that knocked the cigar out of Gleede's mouth, the Jeep came to a stop. From the outside, it seemed as if the earth had suddenly swallowed the front of the car, leaving only the rear end visible. The Jeep's two occupants found themselves leaning forward at an awkward angle. Peering through the windshield, Gleede saw nothing but white directly in front of the headlight beams.

Roderick gave a whistled signal. It was okay to come out of hiding. When the other Ski Troopers saw what had taken place, they jumped up and down and hugged each other.

"It worked!" Brad shouted. "Our second line of defense worked!"

Chapter Seventeen

Roderick was jumping up and down for more than one reason on that cold night. He had turned out to be right, which is important when you think you're a natural-born leader.

Earlier in the evening, he had begun to worry. What if the wall of snow the Ski Troopers had piled up and packed at the bottom of the driveway did not stop Gleede? "We need a little extra insurance," he had decided. Brad had agreed, and contributed some fancy touches of his own.

The "extra insurance" — and second line of defense — was a giant version of the snow pit in Roderick's front yard that had swallowed Freddy Keezer. But it had to be a very special pit. "If it's going to work," Brad had said, switching to his engineer's talk, "we have to build it with a margin of safety. This is no time to..."

"I know," Roderick said. "No time to cut corners."

The way to make sure the snow pit worked, Brad had decided, was to put it just 100 feet from Amelia Higgins's house. At that point, the driveway passed between three-foot banks. The banks, made higher than usual by ridges of plowed snow, formed two ready-made sides of a snow pit.

There was a problem, though. A Jeep couldn't step into a hidden hole as Freddy had done. It had to roll in on wheels. So the Ski Troopers had to build a huge ramp of packed snow that gradually rose before dropping off steeply. This was the "little rise" Gleede noticed as his car was nearing Amelia Higgins's house.

Preparing the trap had taken an awesome amount of shoveling and packing by Roderick's "army." Once it was ready, the Ski Troopers had placed branches across the top and concealed them with loose snow.

No doubt about it, the snow pit worked. You could tell that from the tortured-sounding groans of the Jeep's motor as Gleede tried to back out of the hole. He looked at Lester Ellis in desperation as he kept his foot on the gas. All four wheels spun with a crazy buzzing sound against snow that the Ski Troopers had packed hard for extra slipperiness — another one of Brad's touches.

Brad liked what he saw. "That Jeep won't be going anywhere tonight," he said with a grin.

On the front seat of the Jeep, its driver had reached the same conclusion. Augustus Gleede was seething with anger. Somebody, he didn't know who, had created another obstacle. The time had come, he decided, when even he would have to get out and walk. But getting out did not look easy. The door would open only a few inches before it bumped against packed snow. Gleede banged the door repeatedly against the white wall, with no success.

"We're caught here!" he gasped. "We'll freeze to death!" Then, remembering Freddy and his pals, who had begun to leave, he lowered the side window and yelled: "Come back! Dig us out!"

Kids soon arrived at the edge of the trap, but not the ones Gleede had called. Roderick, Brad, and the other Ski Troopers had come over to gaze at their prisoner. Gleede didn't realize this was a different bunch until Roderick spoke. Standing above the Jeep's driver with his hands on his hips, the chairman of the Ski Troop said triumphantly:

"Well, Mr. Gleede, we've got you where we want you."

"What's going on here!" the driver roared through the side window.

Awkwardly, he strained his head out and upward for a view but was blinded by several flashlights aimed at his face. "Who are you!" he demanded to know. "Who paid you to commit this outrageous act?"

Roderick proudly revealed his name. "Nobody paid us a penny, Mr. Gleede," he said. "We did it for the good of Lysander. You've been ripping off people in this town, but this is one time you won't get away with it. Soon it will be midnight, too late for you to steal Miss Higgins's property from her and sell it for a taco house. And it serves you right!"

"Yeah, yeah, it serves you right," repeated the other Ski Troopers. They broke into laughter and let out joyous whoops.

Gleede turned to his lawyer and said, breathing heavily: "I know who the ringleader is. It's that know-it-all kid from my neighborhood who was on television." Then he remembered that he had refused to let this same kid and a friend shovel his sidewalk.

"Ringley, you're doing this to get even!" Gleede shouted into the darkness, his bushy eyebrows as high as they could go on his furrowed forehead. "I'll have you and these other hoodlums put in the juvenile prison!"

The Ski Troopers grinned and poked each other in the ribs. "Once the clock reaches twelve," Brad said, "we don't care what happens!" Holding his watch under another Ski Trooper's flashlight, he said in a singsong voice: "Only ten minutes left, Mr. Gleede. You'll just have to sit there until the time runs out."

Gleede, however, was not ready to give up within 100 feet of his prize. "Help!" he yelled to the real hoodlums, hoping they were close enough to hear. "Get us out of here! I'll pay four times the usual rate!"

He nearly shouted himself hoarse. Slowly it dawned on Freddy and his pals, down near the entrance to the driveway, that something was wrong.

"I guess he's got a problem," Freddy said in a bored-sounding voice as he lit a cigarette.

"Yeah," said Jimmy Dolan, a skinny, dark-haired boy with a mouth full of bubblegum. "Maybe we better go see."

Seeing the five big, rough-looking boys walking up the driveway, Roderick and his friends quickly disappeared into the snow tunnels.

"Start digging fast!" Gleede shouted as Freddy leaned into the pit to investigate. "We need to get the car doors open!"

"But Mr. Gleede," said Jimmy, who was blowing bubbles, "won't that scratch the paint on your nice car?"

"Who cares about that, you numbskull! Get to work!"

Once again, Freddy Keezer's work crew was not the most efficient one around. In the narrow space around the blocked car doors, the boys got in each other's way. Insults and curses flew, and a lot of snow landed where it wasn't supposed to.

This time the rescuers had an added handicap. They had to work under the greatest bombardment of snowballs they had ever seen. The Ski Troopers had not run away like cowards. They had gone to an underground ammunition supply.

In the moonlight, Freddy recognized Roderick and Brad. Throwing down his shovel in a rage, he started making snowballs for a counterattack. But Gleede noticed this and ordered, "Keep shoveling!"

"But we ain't gonna take this from those little..."

Splat! A snowball on the ear prevented Freddy from saying an exceptionally bad word.

"Get us out of here first!" Gleede said. "Then you can do whatever you please."

So Freddy and his crew kept shoveling as they tried to dodge well-aimed snowballs from the Ski Troopers. Freddy's hair and the back of his neck were soon wringing-wet from snowballs and perspiration.

Gleede pushed on the car door. The opening was getting wider.

"Quit shoveling and give me a hand," he said. The door could now be opened partway, and Gleede's head and one of his hands were sticking out clumsily. "Not like that, you dunce!" he shouted as Freddy pulled on the sleeve of his overcoat, raising the coat but not its owner.

After much twisting and straining, Gleede managed to get his arm out of the car, and then both shoulders. As Freddy and a pal pulled on his arms, Gleede tried to get a foothold in the snow on the edge of the pit.

Watching from the entrance to their snow-cave headquarters, Roderick, Brad, and the other Ski Troopers saw Gleede's head appear above the snow. It was now very close to midnight. The Ski Troopers were as tense as basketball fans in a game that is nearly over.

"There are forty seconds left," Roderick said. "Come on, Mr. Gleede, slip and fall back into that hole!"

As if in answer to a prayer, Gleede tumbled back as his helpers lost their grip. "Quick!" he shouted. "Try again!" On the other side of the car Lester Ellis, twenty years younger than Gleede and nimbler, was already out of the pit. Meanwhile Amelia Higgins, who had finally heard the commotion on her driveway, was turning on lights and peering through parted curtains. Having no idea what was going on, she had called the police. A patrol car would try to get there, she was told.

With Freddy Keezer and a pal bracing their feet against the car and pulling hard, Gleede once again got his head above the snow. Then came his shoulders. Finally, he swung one foot above the snow. "Don't stop pulling!" he said in a voice that showed the effort he was making. His face was red as a beet. "Now, when I say three, pull me up the rest of the way. Ready, one, two..."

As Gleede counted, Roderick also counted — in reverse. "Only twenty seconds to midnight!" he said. "Only fifteen seconds..." Then, as Gleede finally emerged from the pit and paused to catch his breath, Roderick began a countdown, and the other Ski Troopers loudly joined in.

"Five, four, three, two, one! YAAAAAY!"

The roar resounded through the moonlit woods. Roderick and his friends had won. Old Sedgwick was saved! "It's all over, Mr. Gleede!" Roderick shouted. "Kiss that deal goodbye!"

But while Roderick and his friends were going crazy with excitement, Freddy's gang was making snowballs to get revenge. And Gleede was looking at his own watch, which he could see in the bright light from the porch of the old house. Still out of breath, he shouted: "It's not over yet, young man! My watch says I still have one minute." The bank-certified check for $100,000 was in his pocket, ready to be handed over to Amelia Higgins. If he could quickly make it to her door, Gleede figured, her property — and all those profits — would still be his.

He began walking as fast as he could. His well-polished street shoes sank into the snow, but he didn't care.

Twenty seconds went by. Gleede was at the bottom of the porch steps. Lester Ellis was at the door and ringing the bell.

"I'll show the whole conniving bunch of you!" Gleede said. "Nobody's going to stop..."

Whoosh!

Before he could say his name, an unexpected shower of snow forced him to step back. Believing that it had been blown by a gust of wind, he moved again toward the steps...

Whoosh!

Turned back by another curtain of snow, Gleede looked anxiously at his watch. Only twenty seconds to midnight. And this was the real deadline!

Gleede had run into the Ski Troopers' third — and final — line of defense.

Chapter Eighteen

Roderick and the Ski Troopers loudly chanted the new, revised countdown: "Twenty, nineteen, eighteen..." Freddy and his pals, shouting and fighting back with snowballs, contributed to the growing racket.

"C'mon, you're practically there!" Lester Ellis called to Gleede. "What's holding you up?"

"The snow, you imbecile!" Gleede shouted. "The wind's blowing it all over me."

"But the wind stopped hours ago."

"So what's causing it? Aha! I heard you up there!"

Something had dropped on the roof above the porch, causing Gleede to look up. The curtain of snow was coming from kids with shovels! This time the kids were not boys. They were Stacy Zimmermann and Heather Garrity, who had just dropped her shovel.

Early in the evening, they had found Roderick's headquarters by sneaking in behind the Ski Troopers on their way from Crestview Cemetery. After watching for an hour or so while the "army" prepared its defenses, the girls had come out of hiding and offered their help. What could Roderick do? He didn't want to be accused of discriminating against women. So Stacy and Heather became the Ski Troop's first female members.

The best way the girls could help, Roderick had said, was with an "avalanche" in case Gleede got as far as Amelia Higgins's porch steps. In a somewhat embarrassed voice, he explained that it would be like the one he and Bill Goodbody had used on the girls as a joke. Stacy and Heather, who remembered what it was like to have a curtain of snow dropped on them, nudged each other and laughed. "Let's do it!" Stacy had said. Very quietly, using a ladder they found in Amelia Higgins's garage, they had climbed up on the porch roof and waited.

The avalanche now offered the only hope of halting Gleede in the few seconds before midnight.

"Hurry up," Lester Ellis called again to the owner of Hardwick Hardware. "It's now or never." Amelia Higgins, a short, plump woman with a shawl and gold reading glasses, had opened the door. "My stars!" she said as she discovered all the goings-on around her porch. "My stars!"

In the next few moments the fateful day of March 12th came to its official close, and March 13th began. Illuminated by the bright porch light and the boys' glinting flashlights, figures were moving this way and that. So was snow. The Ski Troopers on the ground were now in an all-out snowball battle with Freddy Keezer's gang, which aimed an occasional missile at the girls on the roof. "Dear, dear, dear," said Amelia Higgins, shaking her head. "Dear, *dear!*"

"Here I come," Gleede said. He was frosted all over with snow but wasn't bothering to brush it off.

"Stacy, let him have it!" Roderick shouted to the roof.

The girls flung what seemed like a half-ton of snow over the edge, forcing Gleede to turn back again.

"Six, five, four! ..." chanted the other Ski Troopers, who were dodging snowballs, not always successfully.

"Hurry, hurry!" Lester Ellis yelled, as a badly aimed snowball hit the house within two feet of where he was standing.

"Goodness gracious!" Amelia Higgins said as she ducked behind the front door. Gleede quickly moved toward the porch and reached the first step, then the second...

He was too late.

"Three, two, one, ZERO!!!" the Ski Troopers screamed deafeningly. Up on the roof the girls celebrated by stamping their feet. Briefly ignoring Freddy and his pals, nearly all the Ski Troopers got hit by snowballs.

"Now your time is really up, Mr. Gleede!" Roderick shouted as a snowball socked him on the shoulder. "Mr. Gleede, you have had it! Mr. Gleede, your deal has gone up in smoke!"

No question, midnight had come. But Gleede was not the type who gave up easily.

"Amelia," he said in an unusually humble voice as he reached the front door and Roderick and Brad approached to listen. Gleede spoke loudly and distinctly, so she could hear. "Surely you will overlook the fact that I am a few seconds late," he said, turning on the charm. "That Ringley boy and his young thugs conspired to stop me, Amelia."

The owner of the Sedgwick farmhouse revealed that she, too, had a tough side.

"Don't you 'Amelia' me," she said as a stray snowball landed near Gleede. "I can't say I approve of all the, ahem, methods these youngsters have used. But, Augustus Gleede, you had it coming. You tried to bamboozle me and get this place for nothing." Another snowball landed a few feet away.

"All right, if that's your attitude," Gleede snapped. "I'll take legal action! I'm the victim of a conspiracy by a bunch of young delinquents, and I'll bet the Save Old Sedgwick crowd is in on it too. The courts will hear my case with sympathy..." His voice trailed off, however, when he saw Lester Ellis shaking his head. The lawyer was signaling that Gleede's chances of winning a lawsuit were poor.

Amelia Higgins was looking more and more determined. "As far as

I am concerned," she said, folding her arms, "that option agreement is as dead as my colonial ancestor Zephaniah Sedgwick. I'm now free to sell to anybody I please, for whatever I can get."

Roderick, grinning as he heard this, nudged Brad.

Gleede gave the nice-guy approach another try. "Amelia, listen, please sell the place to me," he said. "I'll raise my price to $200,000."

This offer raised the eyebrows of Amelia Higgins. "That certainly is a lot of money," she said. "Still, I don't like the idea of tearing down my ancestors' home for a taco house..."

"I'll make it $250,000!" Gleede said as a few snowballs kept whizzing nearby.

"My stars! That really is quite a sum."

Just then a man's voice was heard from out in the woods.

"Wait a minute! Hold everything!"

The snowballs stopped. The Ski Troopers aimed flashlights in the direction from which the voice came. They could hardly believe what they saw.

Approaching the house was a sleigh drawn by a horse. In the front seat holding the reins was none other than Ben Drumlin, the carpenter, antiques dealer, and source of Clouds-Go-Wild. Sitting beside him was Vernon Stubbs. On the back seat were Sophie Hopwood and a heavy-set man. Roderick didn't know his name, but his face looked somewhat familiar.

"Be careful what you let him talk you into!" Stubbs shouted as he climbed down from the sleigh. "We have a proposal of our own."

Roderick was astonished to see Ben Drumlin. "I thought you were in Florida," he said.

"If it weren't for all this snow I *would* be in Florida," the carpenter said rather grumpily. When he heard another storm was coming, he said, he had decided to rush back north. "I wanted to make sure the roof didn't collapse and ruin my clock collection."

"Oh, Mr. Gleede," Sophie Hopwood said in her bubbly, low-pitched voice as she climbed down from the sleigh. "We finally have our $350,000! But of course, it's too late to do you any good now. I'm so sorry." As she spoke, her broad smile and perfect teeth were visible in the moonlight.

Then she introduced the other passenger in the sleigh, calling him "this marvelous, public-spirited man. His generous contribution put us way past the finish line!"

The "public-spirited man" was Thornton W. Poindexter, the chairman of a company called Triassic Industries. Just before 11:00, Sophie Hopwood had gone to his house on skis to collect his check for $50,000 because there was no other way to get there in the deep snow. By then, she said, Gleede was not answering his telephone. So she, Vernon Stubbs, and Thornton Poindexter had gone to his house "on this old sleigh, which Ben Drumlin hitched up to a neighbor's horse earlier this evening. But when we came by your house, Mr. Gleede, you were not there!"

This time, Brad nudged Roderick. The other Ski Troopers, including the girls from the roof, had come to the porch to listen. Freddy and his gang were heading home.

"We could have gotten the money to you before midnight, just in the nick of time, Mr. Gleede," said the president of the Save Old Sedgwick committee. "We tried our best to reach you!"

"Well, maybe you did," muttered the owner of Hardwick Hardware, clearly not convinced. "But there's another part I don't get." Gleede turned to Poindexter and asked: "Why on earth would you of all people, a businessman with his head screwed on tight, put up $50,000 for a flea-brained plan to turn this farmhouse into a museum?"

"Part of the reason," Poindexter said in a booming voice, "is oil."

The Ski Troopers gaped at each other.

"My company," the chairman of Triassic Industries explained, "is in the energy business and wants to explore this part of New Jersey. Amelia

Higgins's property is one of the few big pieces of vacant land left in this town." Under a plan worked out that day with the S.O.S. committee, he said, the company would pay $50,000 for the right to bore a deep hole on the property. The purpose, he said, was "purely to have a look at what's down below. If we find anything, whether it's oil or gas, we'll pump it out of the ground from another location." As for the farmhouse, Poindexter added, there would be no damage to "this priceless landmark."

When he had finished talking, Amelia Higgins announced that she would gladly sell her house to the S.O.S. committee for $300,000, "more than I ever dreamed of getting. You can use the other $50,000 you raised to fix up the place." She shook hands with Sophie Hopwood, and the Ski Troopers and other fund-raisers cheered long and loud.

"This is quite a day for the people of Lysander," said the president of S.O.S. with one of her broadest smiles. "We have saved Old Sedgwick in spite of the worst winter in this century."

"With all due respect, I'd like to amend that statement," said Vernon Stubbs as he winked at Roderick and put an arm around his shoulder. "We have saved Old Sedgwick *because* of the worst winter in this century."

Epilogue

Thornton Poindexter's company never found oil or gas under the old Sedgwick Farm, though it certainly tried hard enough. A tall, yellow derrick spent weeks drilling a hole three miles down. But the work crew found something else that settled a 200-year-old question: a British cannonball from the 1700s.

To the citizens of Lysander, this discovery was far more important than oil. Suddenly, real-estate salespersons no longer had to say, "It is strongly believed..." Now they could tell house hunters: "It has been proven that shots were fired in these very streets during the Revolutionary War." Overnight, the value of every home in town — and the commissions charged by real estate firms like Brian O'Meara's — jumped by 20%.

But the Year of the Great Snows, as it came to be called, left a new question. Neighbors still talk and argue about it far into the winter evenings, when fires burn low. Did a local sixth-grader and his friend temporarily have the power to change the weather?

The debate may go on for the next 200 years, because the main piece of evidence is gone.

The last of Clouds-Go-Wild was scattered to the winds on the eve of the final winter storm. The Indian pouch with its cornstalk decorations, which Brad hurled into the woods, was never found. Ben Drumlin, who knew the most about the magic powder, returned to Florida soon after he turned up at Amelia Higgins's farmhouse driving a sleigh. A few months later he died suddenly of a stroke. Roderick Ringley received $100 from a weather research institute for telling what the stuff looked and felt like. But this hardly proved that it was a cloud-seeding substance of amazing potency.

Sweden's Dr. Sven A. Blomquist appeared on a TV science show after writing a long paper on the subject. Once again he declared in his singsong, up-and-down voice that Clouds-Go-Wild could have produced unusually heavy snows — "if the winds were blowing *yoost* the right way and the powder was *yoost* the right kind."

Professor Emerson W. Tippitt refused to take telephone calls from newsmen seeking his comments on Dr. Blomquist's latest remarks. When a TV crew tried to interview Tippitt at an airport, he looked as if he would punch the cameraman.

Whether Roderick was responsible for the big snows or not, everyone around Lysander agrees on one point. His deeds *in* the snow, even if you disapproved of them at the time, made the town a better place. The Indian pouch lured two crooks out of hiding. More important, Roderick and his friends foiled a man who wanted to replace a historic landmark with a Tac-O-Rama fast-food restaurant built in the shape of a sombrero and outlined in red neon lights.

The dedication ceremony for the new colonial museum took place on a warm June day, more than a year after the big blizzard. Roderick was invited to sit in a place worthy of someone who had changed the town's history: right up on the front row of the speaker's platform. He was dressed for a baseball game scheduled to begin right after the ceremony on a new ballfield laid out on part of the property.

On Roderick's left sat Sophie Hopwood, and on his right was Vernon Stubbs. Right behind them sat Brad McCorkle and the rest of the former

Scandinavian Ski Troopers, both female and male. Sergeant Zaremba was a few rows back.

Mayor Winville, re-elected with the help of pictures taken when the President of the United States came to see Lysander's snows, gave a speech that seemed as if it would never end. This caused much fidgeting by Roderick and others eager to start their game.

After that unforgettable night at the farmhouse, Roderick hardly ever talked again about snow. He continued to ski, but his books about mountain climbers and polar explorers gathered dust. Two months after the dedication ceremony, the family passed through Buffalo, New York, on a vacation trip. Dr. Ringley reminded his son that he had once begged to move to a city that gets ninety-five inches of snow a year. Roderick looked embarrassed.

But underneath, the old Roderick was still there. The following January, when he was midway through the eighth grade, his father heard the familiar scraping sound of a shovel after the season's first winter storm.

Watching his son from the bedroom window, Dr. Ringley saw the look of contentment he had seen so many times before. More often than he needed to, Roderick rested while the flakes blew into his face. He looked about in wonder at the new white world that was his alone until others came and made footprints, just as he had looked about on the morning after that first forbidden trip to the hang-glider's cliff.

THE END

About the Author

Born in Philadelphia on Sept. 4, 1927, Edmund Faltermayer earned a Bachelor of Arts Degree with Honors in English from Haverford College in 1949 and a Master of Arts Degree in Russian Studies from Harvard University in 1953. He served in the U.S. Navy from 1953 to 1955, retiring as a lieutenant.

Faltermayer practiced journalism for nearly 50 years. As a staff reporter for *The Wall Street Journal* from October 1955 to June 1963, he covered the Defense Department in Washington D.C. and served as a correspondent in Germany. He made three extensive reporting trips to the former Soviet Union that resulted in more than a score of feature articles, including one in which First Deputy Premier Anastas Mikoyan fumed at America's reluctance to buy his country's goods.

Faltermayer moved to *Fortune* magazine in July 1963, where he served as writer and editor until his death, save for a 16-month stint as an editorial writer and columnist for *Life*, a sister magazine.

Having grown accustomed to the clean streams and neatly manicured parks of Europe, Faltermayer was appalled by the filthy air and garbage-strewn subways he found upon returning to New York City. He vented his outrage in a series of six *Fortune* articles emphasizing the need to clean up the environment. One of them, "We Can Afford Clean Air," was the first to call upon industrial polluters to clean up their act. Faltermayer's series grew into a book, *Redoing America: A Nationwide Report on How to Make Our Cities and Suburbs Livable*, published by Harper & Row in 1968, which was called "impressive" by Senator Edmund Muskie and "direct, practical and down-to-earth" by *The New Yorker*.

More recently, Faltermayer wrote on personal finance ("One Retiree's Nasty Surprises," Dec. 25, 1995), industrial competitiveness ("Invest or Die," cover story, Feb. 22, 1993) and health-care reform ("Will the Cost-Cutting in Health Care Kill You?" Oct. 31, 1994).

He retired from *Fortune's* full-time staff in 1994 and continued as a contributing editor of the magazine's Industrial Management & Technology section until shortly before he died, on Jan. 4, 2003, of complications brought on by Amyotrophic Lateral Sclerosis, also known as Lou Gehrig's disease.

Faltermayer's long-held dream was to publish a novel for children. Inspired by his son Steven's obsession with snow, *Clouds Go Wild* was completed in 2001. A portion of the proceeds from the novel will go to ALS research.